More praise for

ALL IS FORGOTTEN,

NOTHING IS LOST

"The issue here is provocative: to what extent does one's (symbolic or real) intimacy with one's teachers open professional doors—or undermine one's sense of achievement? . . . Bernard and Roman raise questions worthy of Thomas Mann's Adrian Leverkühn, or any thoughtful student or teacher: What is the relationship between talent and craft, genius and mediocrity? Can writing be taught? Does one ever improve?" —*New York Times Book Review*

"A sweet, awkwardly funny, and perfectly true-to-life tale of a group of poets at an MFA program and the people who love them." —Gary Shteyngart, *GQ*

"[Lan Samantha Chang's] characters are three-dimensional and not predictable, and with her simple, elegant style she achieves a clarity that few writers accomplish. . . . Chang is an author worth reading now—and watching in the future." —*Library Journal*

"*All Is Forgotten, Nothing Is Lost* is a small book with a lot of power. . . . With delicate, beautiful prose, and a unique yet oddly familiar story, Chang pierces the depths of friendship, love, art, nostalgia, and regret with breathtaking precision.

This is the kind of novel you can't leave without knowing a little more about yourself."   —Sam Ramos, *Politics & Prose*

"*All Is Forgotten, Nothing Is Lost* offers a starkly honest portrait of people caught up in the drive to write and of the personal bargains and self-deceptions that such an ambition can entail. Lan Samantha Chang was brave to write this book, to turn her novelist's eye onto a world she knows intimately, and her bravery pays off in the unflinching final scenes."
                              —Adam Haslett, author of *Union Atlantic*

"What a lovely, fierce book about love, betrayal, loss, and time's dominion over us all. Fleet, preternaturally attuned to the ebb and flow of personal history, *All Is Forgotten, Nothing Is Lost* is, well, unforgettable. Lan Samantha Chang sees deeply into her characters, right down to their souls, but she wields her intelligence with the compassion of a master."
                              —Scott Spencer, author of *A Ship Made of Paper*

"Lucy, Roman, Bernard, and Miranda are characters you won't soon forget. In their passionate, demanding, wrecked, and joyous literary lives, they thrive on their belief in language's absolute authority. This deeply affecting—and elegant— novel by Lan Samantha Chang definitely offers what Leonard Cohen calls his whole career in song: *All day and night, versions of the erotic.* I wish I could live long enough to discover this novel in an attic trunk a hundred years in the future, and exclaim, so this is what 'poetic education' really meant."
                              —Howard Norman, author of *What Is Left the Daughter*

"The author of this unusual novel sidesteps the arcane for a story that explores the universality of human experience and the inherent self-doubt of creativity. . . . Chang takes the abstract, infuses it with truth and dares us to look the other way." —*Curled Up*

"Lan Samantha Chang's elegant and vivid prose will draw you into this slip of a novel and haunt you long after you read the last page. In *All Is Forgotten, Nothing Is Lost*, Chang tackles some deep questions about writing, art, love, betrayal and self-worth. I love, love, loved this book." —*Dog Ear*

ALL IS FORGOTTEN,

NOTHING IS LOST

ALL IS FORGOTTEN,
NOTHING IS LOST

—

LAN SAMANTHA CHANG

W. W. NORTON & COMPANY

NEW YORK · LONDON

Copyright © 2010 by Lan Samantha Chang

"The Idea of Order at Key West,"from *The Collected Poems of
Wallace Stevens* by Wallace Stevens, copyright 1954 by Wallace
Stevens and renewed 1982 by Holly Stevens. Used by permission
of Alfred A. Knopf, a division of Random House, Inc.

For information about permission to reproduce selections from this
book, write to Permissions, W. W. Norton & Company, Inc.,
500 Fifth Avenue, New York, NY 10110

For information about special discounts for bulk purchases, please
contact W. W. Norton Special Sales at specialsales@wwnorton.com
or 800-233-4830

Manufacturing by Courier Westford
Book design by Barbara Bachman
Production manager: Julia Druskin

Library of Congress Cataloging-in-Publication Data

Chang, Lan Samantha.
    All is forgotten, nothing is lost / Lan Samantha Chang.—1st ed.
        p. cm.
    ISBN 978-0-393-06306-6 (hardcover)
1. Poets—Fiction. 2. Poetry—Authorship—Fiction. 3. Teacher–
student relationships—Fiction. 4. Triangles (Interpersonal
relations)—Fiction. 5. Psychological fiction. I. Title.
PS3553.H2724A79 2010
813'.54—dc22
                                                                2010017503

ISBN 978-0-393-34056-3 pbk.

W. W. Norton & Company, Inc.
500 Fifth Avenue, New York, N.Y. 10110
www.wwnorton.com

W. W. Norton & Company Ltd.
Castle House, 75/76 Wells Street, London W1T 3QT

1 2 3 4 5 6 7 8 9 0

For Rob

PART ONE

A POETIC EDUCATION

——

MIRANDA STURGIS WAS AN EXCEPTIONAL POET. AMONG the School's distinguished faculty, she was the brightest star, and graduate students fought to gain admission to her seminars. It was 1986, and the most fervent feared they had missed the age of poetry—that they were born into the era of its decline. To Miranda and the School they came in defiance of that decline; or, at the very least, to sit for two years in the circle of her radiance. They yearned to know her mind and hoped to earn her blessing as they set forth on an uncertain path.

But Miranda was critical of their work and dismissive of their hopes. She rarely offered praise. She discussed their poems ruthlessly, as if they were not in the room. Of the students in her classes, almost none escaped unaltered or unscathed, and some stopped writing altogether. Such was her teaching that the students at the School had invented a special nickname for her critiques: they were called bludgeonings, as in, "He's drunk. He's just been bludgeoned."

Out in the world—the small, passionate world of poetry—Miranda maintained a sterling reputation as a teacher. There was learning and acuity in her body of work: the shimmering debut; the rigorous and ambitious second book; the third book short-listed for several major national prizes. She was considered an accurate and influential judge of talent. It was rumored that she sometimes took a special interest in the career of a young poet, and that her protégés began with a vital advantage. And so, despite the bludgeonings, despite confusion and hurt feelings, the students kept lining up to take her classes. They concealed their discouragement from their families, most of whom did not read poetry; from the School, of whose faculty she was by no means the worst instructor; and from Miranda herself, because they sensed, with the visceral knowledge of neglected children, that if they were to complain to her, she would not notice. Instead, they watched her keenly. They studied how she dressed and how she did her hair. They puzzled over the hesitant yet determined way she gestured as she spoke. They tried to copy these habits as if they could learn to *be* Miranda—could transform their own young hands, grasping their pens, into her delicate, reluctant hands.

ROMAN MORRIS WAS a student in Miranda's seminar. He was twenty-eight, slightly older than those who arrived at the School fresh from undergraduate study, but he had the same hopes and expectations as they. Or perhaps his expectations were even greater. For three years after college he had worked at a small private bank, and had quit that lucrative job in order to pursue the art of poetry.

Roman had tried to get into Miranda's seminar the previous spring. He had expressed his interest openly by putting notes—quoting her poems—into her mailbox. He was shunted off into the class of another professor. As a result of this dismissal, he had developed what he thought a healthy objectivity, and he had coined the term "acolyte" to describe those classmates—mostly young women—who hung on Miranda's every word. He saw himself as an observer, and had concluded that he would keep his own poems from his classmates, would wait until he had assessed how his work would be received.

Objectivity aside, he did not know what to make of Miranda. He had never before sought, and still failed to receive, a teacher's attention. He had never encountered a professor so unwilling to be known. Was she indifferent to them, or was she guarding her privacy? Was she cruel, or simply telling them the truth?

It was November, the tenth week of the term, and the seminar room grew dark by late afternoon. The long table sat a dozen, with Miranda at the head. From his place at the other end, Roman watched his classmates' cigarette smoke rise and disappear into the gloom, which gradually dimmed their faces and hands until the only clear shapes were their white paper cups of wine. No one turned on the light. Miranda loathed fluorescent lighting. In the winter she generally let things go until the break and held the rest of the class by candlelight.

They were discussing a draft of Bernard Sauvet's historical poem on the exploration of Wisconsin. Bernard had turned in the poem after more than a year of drafting and revision; he and Roman had spent hours discussing its form and content. Bernard was not allowed to respond when his poem was being critiqued. He sat beside Roman, visibly trembling, his flushed cheeks fogging his wire-rimmed glasses.

With the instinct of ambition, Roman had identified the skinny and reserved Bernard as one of the most serious poets in their class. He believed his friend was a sincere poet; a hopeful poet; and—if there were such a thing—an honest poet. Now he began to say as much, but was silenced by a fierce glare from Phebe Platz. Point by point, the acolytes went on with their critique. The poem was overly lyrical; it was not lyrical enough. The poem did not reference history; it was too historical. The poem lacked essential irony; the poem was a farce. Each speaker directed her comments at Miranda, who gazed thoughtfully ahead, lacing her fingers over the manuscript. Her silver wedding ring glinted faintly in the dusk. Several times, Roman wondered if she might be looking at him, but careful inspection revealed that she was actually focused on a point in space somewhere above his left ear.

She was a slender woman with dark, unruly curls she usually wore twisted into a knot. Roman wondered if he would find it easier to put up with her indifference if she were less attractive. He thought her steadily maturing author photographs were sexy, but he found her more disturbing in the flesh. She was aware of her appeal, and used it as a screen; her pose of coolness, he suspected, was probably a sham, and possibly an attempt to hide that she found teaching very dull indeed.

After twenty minutes, she yawned. The yawn was violent and egregious, made more unforgivable, Roman thought, by the girlish way she covered her mouth with both hands, as if she thought it possible to conceal the boredom she felt upon encountering Bernard's inner life. A curl sprang onto her forehead. Her hair was the one part of her that resisted elegance.

The acolytes took note. "What do you think, Miranda?" Phebe asked, and the others joined in. "Tell us what you think."

Miranda shrugged. Raising her eyes, she gazed out over the table. She shook her head briefly, dismissing the poem, and Bernard, and possibly, thought Roman, all of them.

"I think Bernard has heard enough today," she said.

The students put down their pens.

They turned to a poem written by a very shy, plump, black-clad young woman named Shannon Bruno. Shannon's poem, "The Visiology of Confinement," was unusual in its use of white space, in its fragmented lines eliding punctuation. The acolytes spoke admiringly of its originality, its edginess. They praised its abstruseness and what Phebe called "the intention of its meaninglessness." Their conversation grew animated, punctuated by the red tips of their cigarettes as they made brief stabs and gestures in the dimming light.

But at the height of the discussion, Miranda cleared her throat. Instantly, the room grew silent. The students, who had, if it was possible, forgotten that she was there, turned in unison to her end of the table.

For a moment, she did not speak. These hesitations, which often occurred before she said something especially harsh, were a topic of debate among her students. *Why* did she pause? Were the hesitations simply meant to draw attention? Roman was almost certain this was the case. Or were they a sign of true reluctance—as Bernard insisted—born of sympathy, of her memory of a time when she, too, had been young and fragile, struggling to shape words into art?

Miranda picked up the sheet of paper on which Shannon's poem had been typed. Then she released the manuscript. Slowly it drifted down, pale in the dim light, landing silently on the table.

"Is this a poem?" she asked.

Roman peered at her with curiosity. Her expression was rather pained, as if she did not want to ask the question, but felt compelled, by some obligation they could not know, to bring it up.

Miranda tipped her head back and began to speak.

"She sang beyond the genius of the sea.
The water never formed to mind or voice,
Like a body wholly body, fluttering
Its empty sleeves; and yet its mimic motion
Made constant cry, caused constantly a cry,
That was not ours although we understood,
Inhuman, of the veritable ocean."

Roman let out a breath. "The Idea of Order at Key West" was one of his favorite poems.

As she continued to recite the poem, Miranda's voice grew resonant. A rich, fluid clarity—almost like music—filled each line. The whole of her person—hands, hair, voice—was suddenly so real, so more than real, that Roman forgot to think.

He saw a sliver moon rise over the petty lights of his hometown. He was in high school, gazing at the evening sky and yearning for the world. Then he was in a college library, deep in a big chair, reading Wallace Stevens for the first time and knowing that *this* was what he wanted.

Lost in a dream, he only vaguely heard the poem's end: "'And of ourselves and of our origins / In ghostlier demarcations, keener sounds.'" Miranda folded her hands and looked serenely at the class.

No one spoke. The poem had bewitched them and they could not say a word.

For several minutes, they sat in the dark. Then, from somewhere to Roman's left, a precise, reedy tenor voice emerged into the gloom. "'If I read a book—'" the voice began.

Miranda nodded, as if to say, Go on.

"—'and it makes my whole body so cold no fire ever can warm me I know *that* is poetry.'"

It was Bernard, quoting Emily Dickinson's famous lines to Thomas Wentworth Higginson.

"'If I feel physically as if the top of my head were taken off,'" Bernard continued, "'I know *that* is poetry. These are the only way I know it. Is there any other way?'"

Miranda sat up in her chair. It seemed to Roman that she had risen over them, and she hovered there, her pale gray eyes glowing down.

"I feel compelled to say a few things about this work," she said, nodding at Shannon's poem.

"There was a time, decades ago," she said, "when every schoolchild in this country memorized Shakespeare, Blake,

Shelley. We were brought up on the poetry of human experience, and we turned to poets when we sought truth."

She looked over their heads—beyond them, it seemed to
Roman.

"Along with this education came respect for poetic form.
We understood that forms were patterns of human conscious-
ness. Forms of beauty and restraint. Forms that freed our
minds to reach toward the sublime.

"Poets are still living," Miranda said. "But there are fewer
and fewer now, and it seems to many that the art has been
diminished. Some say, because poetry is no longer taught
to children. Some say, because of classes like this one. The
causes are unclear. But it *is* clear that few outside our world
read the poetry now being written. *This poem is one reason
why.*" Her words fell into the room with absolute authority.
"No one would choose to read this; it exists to interest only
its author and"—she looked around—"the author's illustration of prevailing ideas. It is utterly derivative and utterly
unmemorable."

The stillness that followed was as the moment after one has
felt a thud under the wheel of a car in which one is a passenger. In that moment, Roman caught Bernard's wire-rimmed
glasses glinting as he looked up at Miranda; he saw voyeurism
on the faces of the acolytes; he saw Shannon drop her head
into her hands. Shannon's fingernails were painted blue, but
in the twilight they looked black.

Miranda glanced at the clock, her mouth suddenly weary.
In a more thoughtful teacher, Roman guessed, it might have
been an expression of regret.

"Class dismissed," she said. She picked up her bag and exited the room. Her heels clicked down the hall and then there was more silence.

No one knew what to do. Lucy Parry, who was the youngest and prettiest girl in the class, turned to Shannon and tried to say something, but Shannon shook her head. And so the others pushed back their chairs. They picked up their books and coats, winding their scarves around their necks, fishing in their pockets for their lighters and cigarettes. They turned and filed out.

The room was almost dark. From where Shannon was huddled came a series of choking sobs. Roman looked away. He had no desire to shun her; yet he felt contempt for her, and shame.

He sat and waited for Bernard. The origin of their friendship lay in conversations after class, as they were the only male students who did not smoke.

Bernard zipped his pencils back into their case. He put the copies of his own poem back into his worn valise. Then he rose, slowly, deliberately, went around the table, and touched a narrow fingertip to Shannon's quivering shoulder. "It wasn't personal," he offered timidly. "She didn't mean you. She was mourning our diminished world, that's all; not scolding you."

Shannon nodded, rubbing her eyes and nose upon her sleeve. After a minute or two, she stood up, put on her coat, and, clutching her arms around her chest, followed the others out of the room.

Roman waited for her footfalls to fade. Then he flipped on the light.

"Jesus Christ," he said, an expression he knew upset Bernard. "She was 'mourning our diminished world'?"

Bernard put his valise on the table and sat back down. He propped both elbows on the valise, then looked up at Roman, blinking. His bright blue eyes shone through his glasses. "I think Miranda liked my poem," he said. "Did you notice how she did?"

Then, as Roman waited with growing frustration, Bernard reached into his valise and pulled out an orange.

Art made strange allies. Aside from a love of poetry and an abjuration of cigarettes, Roman had nothing in common with his closest friend at the School. Bernard was a mild young man of thirty-one who already behaved as if he were middle-aged. He told Roman he read Proust each evening until ten o'clock and went to sleep. Bernard appeared to have no interest in fame or worldly achievement. For more than a year, he had been working doggedly on his poem, "All Is Forgotten, Nothing Is Lost," told from the point of view of Louis Joliet, the French fur trapper, who, along with Father Jacques Marquette, a Jesuit missionary, had paddled and portaged through the wetlands of his home state. The class had decided the poem was homoerotic in a painfully repressed but beautiful way. They had debated whether its theme was meant to be the nature of transgression. From his window overlooking St. Joseph's Cathedral, Roman had often glanced down onto the street and seen his slight, beaky friend, wearing always the same red tie and gray cardigan sweater, making his way to mass on Sundays and Wednesdays. Presumably he confessed his sins, most likely sins only in the imagination.

As far as Roman could tell, the poem had nothing to do with transgression. Bernard was too virtuous to write about transgression. Even his refusal to smoke seemed to grow out of an ideal of purity that had its roots in a source too violent and extreme for easy comprehension.

"Did you notice?" Bernard repeated.

"I noticed Miranda must have her period today," Roman said.

Bernard gave him a bleak look.

"It was unfortunate," said Bernard, "but I don't believe her comments were meant personally. She was truly thinking about the world."

"That's crap," Roman said. He drew a breath that filled his lungs. It was the first time that he—or anyone in class, he thought—had put into words what he was about to say.

"She's a great poet," he said, "but a poor teacher. I bet she spends more time every day choosing her shoes than reading our poems."

Bernard sat, orange in hand, flushing to his hairline.

Roman went on. "What was the point of her beating up Shannon like that? It's not her favorite kind of poetry—it's not mine, either—but is it right to blast someone for their *vision*? Not for their poor execution of their vision—but for the vision itself?"

Bernard examined his orange. "Is this the reason you haven't shown the class any of your work?"

"No. Of course not." Roman cleared his throat. He was the only member of the class who had not turned in a poem; most had done it at least twice, and a few put something forward almost every week.

"I don't think you should withhold your work. You will miss something very valuable," said Bernard, quietly but with conviction.

"Thanks for the advice."

"I would like very much to discuss this more—you've raised some fascinating questions about art and teaching. Perhaps we should wait until the post-critique?" He meant the bar.

"I might not go today," Roman searched for an excuse. "I have to make a phone call."

"Your grandmother? Let's talk later then. I'm so excited by Miranda's reaction to my own poem that I should wait to formulate my thoughts."

Roman shook his head. "Bernardo. How do you know she even read your poem?"

Bernard fished out a manuscript from his valise, turned it over, and pointed. Roman squinted, leaning forward. On the bottom of the final page, Miranda had written in her loopy, vague script: *Hmmm.*

Roman squelched a flicker of envy. "Bernardo," he said, "aren't you pissed off? You've been working on that poem for fourteen months."

"Not at all," said Bernard, putting his thumb into the orange peel. A true devotee, he spoke of Miranda's flaws as if they were foibles. "I didn't come to this seminar with the goal of making her recognize my talent. Contrary to what most of the class believes, it's far more important for the young poet to see the great one than for the great poet to see the younger one."

Roman considered this remark. "What kind of sour-grapes bullshit is that?"

"We should think about what her indifference means." Carefully, Bernard broke off a piece of his orange. "What might be learned from the indifference of a great poet. Would you like some of my orange? It's good."

Roman refused the orange.

HE WALKED HOME through downtown Bonneville, avoiding his classmates at the bar and in particular avoiding Phebe Platz. He wondered why Miranda had let her into the seminar. Phebe was an unremarkable poet he had dated briefly the year before, who had taken the short affair too seriously and lied to everyone about it. What to him seemed a cursory error, made before he understood the stifling social networks of his classmates, had determined his reputation among the acolytes. They considered him a playboy and an unsupportive male, narcissistic and uninterested in the writing of women. They assumed it was Miranda's sexiness and fame alone that had brought him to her class. That he actually read the poetry of women; that he had read and admired Miranda's work; that he had nothing, in fact, against Phebe, except that she had spoken ill of him: all of this carried scant weight with the acolytes.

To avoid Oscar's, the student bar, he walked east of the courthouses and into the commercial heart of Bonneville, cutting straight through the glass lobby of the actuarial firm established by the School's late founder, Angus P. McManus. McManus, a weekend poet, had left his entire personal fortune to his small, private alma mater, "for the purpose of establishing a Program of the Poetic Arts offering a graduate degree, independent from the College and yet allowing its students access to its privileges." The McManus lobby was imposing. At a certain time of evening, in a certain light, Roman could sometimes imagine that he had stepped into the glass and steel tower in Boston where he had once worked. Now, he was suddenly aware of his image reflected back at him from all sides: a tall, reliably handsome and dark-haired young man, too old to be a student, dressed as a student nonetheless. He hurried to the street.

When he first took his banking job, it had all seemed possible. Hadn't T. S. Eliot worked in business? For three years, Roman sent his shirts to the cleaners and paid off the mortgage for his grandmother, Emily. He read and wrote as much as he could. But as poetry was pushed more and more underground, he became aware of a low-level disturbance, an illness, that crept into his body and mind until a heavy misery confronted him each morning upon waking.

And so he began a life fully committed to poetry. He gave up a secure salary, a finite list of duties, in exchange for two years in Bonneville, Michigan, and, following this, no clear path.

Roman crossed a block of restaurants, then a street of

auto repair shops, entering the shabby neighborhood where he lived. The seminar had left him both exhilarated by and angry with Miranda Sturgis. She made, he knew, a generous salary. Angus P. McManus had made certain she would never be in want. She was one of many poets who were able to take their living for granted. Previous generations had been shielded from the grimy world of counting change. Robert Browning and Elizabeth Barrett, Amy Lowell, Gertrude Stein, T. S. Eliot: all had come from wealth. Even Emily Dickinson, he thought, remembering Bernard's rapturous quotation, had been able to live comfortably in the home of her well-established Amherst family.

Roman was also paid for teaching, though considerably less than Miranda. Three times a week, he met an undergraduate composition class. He found little pleasure in teaching, but was mindful of his responsibilities. Was not Miranda, likewise, being paid to lavish attention on her students—to nurture the young poets who sought to follow in her footsteps? Should she not, at least, make an effort to care about them and their work? Or what if Bernard was correct, and they were all meant to learn from her exactly as she was? Roman did not want her to critique his poems. Perhaps Bernard was right about this, too: perhaps Roman was afraid to hear what Miranda might say.

Roman jammed his fists into his pockets. But he *must* show her his poems. For he had glimpsed it in her face: the partiality he craved. She had grown so pure and alive as she recited Stevens. He imagined her eating lunch alone with winter sunlight filtering through the window, reading her tattered copy of *Ideas of Order* as she poked at a few lettuce leaves absentmindedly with chopsticks. What was she like, behind that fiercely guarded privacy; what did she *want*?

With some dismay, he recognized that he had lost his objectivity. From this evening, Roman—no more the observer, no better than the rest of them—would work and wait for the rare and indisputable moment when Miranda might encounter a stanza or a line—even a few words—of his poetry that she admired.

ROMAN LIVED IN A SHABBY back apartment. To save money, he never left the light on for himself, and he had to feel his way up the outdoor stairs in order to keep from stepping between the wooden slats. He would not take comfort in the banality of the present, but would instead continue striving, with all of the energy and confidence he could muster, for the as yet unseen magnificence of the future. The inside of his apartment was almost bare. It could have been a furnished rental but for the sleek telephone and answering machine he had purchased during his years as a banker. On his writing table, he had taped a note the size of a fortune cookie message. The note read, *All that matters is the work*.

At eight o'clock, when the rates went down for the evening, Roman dialed his grandmother's number. For days, he had been willing himself to return her calls.

The phone began to ring. Roman envisioned Emily, five hundred miles away, slowly making her way over the braided rugs, around the rocking chair, to where the phone sat on an old telephone table. He braced himself for the sound of her voice: a melodious, utterly changeable and unpredictable, faintly Southern sound. She was always happy to hear from him. "Roman! Roman, is that you? How are you doing, honey?"

"I'm fine."

"Did you write a poem today?"

Roman did not reply. Emily seemed to think that he should sit down and write a poem each morning after brushing his teeth. Her favorite poet was Longfellow, whose work was given slight attention by the professors at the School.

"Have you decided where you're going at the end of the year? Are you coming home? Or back to Boston?"

"I may have mentioned this before," Roman said, slowly, for in fact, he had not. "I'm applying for some fellowships. So I don't know where I'll be going."

"How about Thanksgiving?" When he did not reply immediately, she added, in a coaxing tone, "I'm making charlotte russe."

This Thanksgiving tradition was an utterly un-Thanksgiving-like dessert: a light, fragrant white cake, served with a heady crème, and a luscious red fruit sauce redolent of liqueur. It was a recipe from her childhood in Baton Rouge, and although Roman knew almost nothing of the Southern family for whom he had been named, a mouthful of the charlotte russe called to mind an imaginary luxury for which he felt nostalgic.

"I can't," he said.

This was a lie, and the empty line hummed with their

knowledge of it. No matter that she had taught him that white lies were permissible, if they spared the feelings of others.

"Is it the money?" Her voice was charming, innocent, as if she were a source of money absolutely bottomless. "How much do you need?"

"I don't want to take your money."

"You could ride the bus." This was true—and if he were a more faithful grandson, a better person, perhaps he might. "The bus isn't so bad, Roman. The trick—there's a trick, you know—is that you must make certain you sit down next to someone instead of taking an empty seat. That way you get to choose whom you ride next to."

There was something conspiratorial in her tone. For a moment, Roman allowed himself to believe in the conspiracy, to imagine that through her method, the long ride might be made cozy and secure, its misery banished by her ingenuity. But she had told him the bus trick half a dozen times, beginning ten years before when he had first left her for college.

Her optimism, her belief that there was always a special way for him, had buoyed him as a child; then, when he grew older and understood that she would someday die, it had begun to fill him with anxiety. She had raised him on expectations and had left him now, in his late twenties, alone in the world with his ambition.

"You don't want to come home," Emily said sadly. "Not now and not after graduation."

He pictured her sitting in the small house, every window lit up to combat the encroaching misery of winter in western Massachusetts, every cubbyhole crammed with glowing houseplants. Roman had never known his father, and his mother had left the two of them when he was three. Emily had seemed to survive that first departure and had thrown herself into knitting, but fifteen years later, she had taken poorly his leaving for college. The house had become more cluttered with each infrequent visit. Most recently, she had taken to feeding stray cats, an infuriating, clichéd illustration of her loneliness that offended and hurt Roman to the point where he could hardly bear to think of returning.

"I'm sorry I can't give you what you need," Emily said. "I lie awake at night wishing I'd been able to give you the kind of life you want your life to be."

What, Roman wondered as he replaced the receiver, would his grandmother have made of the discussions in that evening's seminar?

WORKING ALONE OVER Thanksgiving break, it seemed to Roman that he heard a man and a woman speaking in his mind. Listening to them felt intimate and strange, like eavesdropping on conversation between a couple lying in the dark. He began to write down their words, to shape them. The process, haunting and deeply confusing, made him wish that he could clear out all distractions and do nothing else. If only he did not have to worry about money; if only he did not have to teach or go to seminar: perhaps he would be able to write something truly—what did he mean? Truly, truthfully?

Roman spent Thanksgiving with Bernard, whose own solitude and poverty were, at such times, a comfort. Bernard lived in an attic room so small that it was not a legal apartment, but was rented only through word of mouth. In the narrow, slanted room, he had a closet and a child-sized bed under the eave, a window that looked upon the roof of the Laundromat, a TV tray where he ate his meals, and a tall, battered black filing cabinet he had dragged home from the university surplus store. A tiny picture of the Virgin Mary hung over his bed. On the filing cabinet stood a figurine of Christ, in white robes, with his hands outstretched, his bare feet resting on a doily that had been crocheted, Bernard explained, by his late great-aunt Katharine. The rest of the room was taken over by books. Lines of books stacked, spine-outward, on the wooden floor up to the bottom of the window; rows of books on a makeshift shelf of planks and cinder blocks; dozens of books piled on his bed, against the wall, leaving only a narrow space for Bernard to sleep and read.

Roman and Bernard shared a meal of grilled cheeses, made under Bernard's ancient flatiron; a bottle of cheap wine; and, in a nod to Thanksgiving custom, apple turnovers from the nearby fast food place, which stayed open on major holidays until late afternoon.

After an initial year of caution, Roman had understood that Bernard could be counted upon not to exploit their friendship: that is, not to assume any unreasonable loyalties, not to cling, and not (for Roman was uncertain of Bernard's preferences) to fall in love. In his eccentric and hidden way, Bernard was trustworthy. Some of this, Roman knew, came from an innate sense of consideration. Bernard would not take his own problems out on others. It was a considerateness he himself had never felt the need to practice, so he admired it; and if it might also have its shadow—in a stubborn and unrealistic expectation of certain people and ideas, in a rigidity of judgment—Roman knew that the considerateness kept him safe from those darker elements, for now.

He had been to Bernard's room on only two previous occasions, and this afternoon he indulged his curiosity. "What's in the filing cabinet, Bernardo? Your ancestral bones?"

Startled, Bernard looked up from the delicate operation of extracting melted cheese from the bottom of his iron. Roman thought about the instinct that had made him refrain from asking this question before. What could be in the cabinet? he wondered. Pornography? Even less likely: love letters?

"It's correspondence," Bernard said finally.

Roman waited. Clearly there was more to come. "So you're sending out your poems?"

A blush spread over Bernard's cheeks and into his forehead. "I am corresponding," he said, "with the writers of our time."

"Is that why you live in this awful place? Is it the cost of stamps?"

"Postage does cost money," Bernard admitted.

There was another silence, and Roman heard the creak of the pipes from downstairs as Bernard's landlady flushed the toilet.

"True poets and writers are alive today," Bernard said. He looked out the window at the succession of tin and tiled roofs that made up his view. "I would like to know them. About ten years ago, in my early twenties, I began to write letters of admiration to the writers I respected. Some of them actually responded, with generosity and insight. And so I have become a pen pal of sorts."

"Franz Xaver Kappus," Roman said.

"Yes. Except that I never burden them with my work, as he did to Rilke. They have plenty of other things to read. And their words on any subject are valuable."

"Unless, as Miranda says, they and everything they ever wrote will be forgotten."

Bernard said, "I don't mean that they are valuable in terms of money."

They sat for a moment in silence. A couple of pigeons, mating or fighting, fluttered outside the window.

"Miranda did not say that they would be forgotten," Bernard pointed out. "She said that they were not being as widely read. Miranda said that fewer poets are being read, but she did not say that *we* should not read them, or remember them."

Roman was impressed by the precision of Bernard's memory. "Will you use the letters somehow in your own work?" he asked.

"No," said Bernard.

"But what exactly is the purpose of your correspondence?" Although the question felt unkind, Roman could not help asking.

Bernard answered, serenely, "I don't know."

They went together to the files. Only one drawer was needed, Bernard explained; but he had gotten the big cabinet for nothing. Bernard had arranged the letters according to some mysterious order. Roman glanced in a hanging folder marked "deceased." There were several files inside. "Ted Berrigan. Richard Brautigan. John Ciardi," he read. "Who was John Ciardi?"

"He wrote an excellent translation of *The Divine Comedy* that I read in college."

"Brion Gysin, Archibald MacLeish. Your aesthetic is all over the place. Isn't Gysin one of Shannon Bruno's experimental heroes?"

"I suppose he would be. I first wrote to him in my twenties, when I was forming my opinions, reading more widely than I'm reading now. He was a nice man. He wrote me back three times."

"And Brautigan?" Roman knew that Richard Brautigan had shot himself in the head with a .44 Magnum, just a few years before, while gazing out at the Pacific Ocean. They had not discovered his body for six weeks.

Bernard shook his head, ruefully. "Schizophrenia, alcoholism, severe depression. No response."

"Berrigan?"

"Flat broke, hepatitis, addicted to amphetamines. No response."

The novelists, it seemed, were faring better than the poets. Roman looked through their files: Shirley Hazzard, William Maxwell, Thomas Pynchon, Marilynne Robinson, Wallace Stegner, John Valentine—

"Who is John Valentine?"

Bernard sat back on his heels. "He wrote a marvelous, very brief first novel called *Open Ends*—clearly autobiographical—about the friendship he developed with his lieutenant en route to the Asian theater in World War II. It's just wonderful—doesn't mention the war, except in incidental ways, and yet it's extraordinarily haunting. A kind of love story, really. When I read it, I just had to write him a letter. And he wrote back. It turns out he attended the School. After Princeton, and World War II, he came here to study poetry for a year on the GI Bill, but never graduated. He married a very rich woman instead, and worked unsuccessfully in advertising, and there were two children, and a divorce—his wife remarried a surgeon. He said his was a marriage that did not survive his determination to make a life as a writer. He didn't finish a novel until he was forty-five years old, and he still hasn't achieved much commercial recognition."

Bernard filed the novelists back into the drawer. "He has a rather pessimistic outlook on relationships. He says, 'The price of art is sadness.' That a person should be very careful whom he loves, and that above all, he should never mix love and debt. I understand, of course, that Mr. Valentine's a rather wounded man. Perhaps too sensitive a man to live comfortably in our time."

Roman wondered how Bernard could feel such generosity and acceptance toward this minor writer he'd never met. As on several other occasions, he was puzzled by the pointlessness of the pursuits to which Bernard devoted all of his spare time apart from his own writing, rather than applying for jobs or fellowships, or sending out his poems. "Bernard," Roman said, "what are your plans for the future?"

"The future?" Bernard said. He had been scanning the

files so intently, Roman realized, that Bernard had forgotten all about him.

"For your life, after we graduate, in less than six months."

"My life?" Bernard looked puzzled. "I suppose that I will move to New York City and continue doing what I'm doing."

Roman felt vaguely envious; he had not known Bernard was capable of such a desire. "Why New York?"

Bernard pondered the question for a moment. "I suppose that I have always liked the idea of living in New York—in a small apartment, a modest place like this one, a walk-up, of course. And you? What are your plans?"

Roman shrugged. "To become a great poet," he said, trying to make it sound like a joke, although he was far from joking.

Bernard waited, his blue eyes expectant. In the pause that followed, Roman felt a warning fissure, as from a temblor, in the foundation of self-confidence upon which he depended so much. He took a deep breath and willed his mind to a brief flight from his own apprehension—to a future when he would have made his mark: when he would look back upon these student days, this squalor, with fond indifference.

After a few moments, Bernard let the subject drop. It was one of the qualities that endeared him to Roman: Bernard did not seem to think that making plans was necessary, nor was asking probing questions. One followed one's interests: that was all.

Roman planned. He had his own filing cabinet, only two

drawers, filled with records of poems submitted to journals, marked with dates of submission, acceptances, and rejections. In his years at the School, he had placed more than a dozen poems in literary magazines. He approached the entire enterprise with a keen eye to strategy and organization. At the School, strategy was said not to matter, only talent; and yet strategy *must* matter—Roman knew it must. There was such a thing as genius, and there was also such a thing as a combination of strategy and talent, and only the great, secret judges of poetry would be honest enough, in the end, to tell the difference. Who these great and secret judges were, he was not certain. But he believed that somehow, somewhere, they were living, and that they would judge him, Roman, favorably. With this belief in mind, he searched through the biographies of poets for patterns, portents; in his professors, he craved evidence of extreme and rigorous standards. But just in case he might be wrong, and they were not living— and in case the great index finger from above did not descend and point him out—he kept his files and made his plans.

He said to Bernard, "If you don't want to teach, and aren't worried about publication, why did you come to the School?"

"Well . . . ," Bernard began. He sat back on his heels again and gazed out the little window, over the back alley with its dilapidated wall, beyond the modest old frame houses filled to the brim with visiting children and extended family members, and beyond their fenced yards, each with its own barking dog chained away from the festivities, gnawing its own Thanksgiving bone. It seemed to Roman that Bernard saw beyond all of this—not exactly as if he were looking toward some spiritual ideal, but in a similar way, as if he had transplanted his religiosity into the thought he was about to share with Roman.

"I came here looking for my One Great Reader," he said.

"What do you mean by that?"

"I mean the one person to whom I write, whom I will imagine as the ideal witness for my artistic life and work."

"And have you found this person?" Roman asked.

"Yes."

He spoke with a fervency to which teasing was the only plausible response. "Will I see her at the holiday dance?"

"Perhaps," said Bernard, and smiled a little smile of happiness and privacy. Roman squelched another of the odd moments of jealousy he sometimes felt around his friend. Never mind that the idea was crackpot, or that the ideal audience might be, from Bernard's point of view, one of the acolytes—certainly, several of the acolytes were attractive girls, desirable, that is, until you got to know them; or the postal carrier who had delivered all of those letters; or a statue of Saint Francis in the cathedral near Roman's apartment. He wanted to guess who this reader was, but Bernard had turned back to the files in such a way that Roman understood he would not entertain speculations or even, perhaps, discuss the matter again.

ROMAN SUBMITTED THREE of his new poems for critique at the final class. They were very good, he believed—far beyond what he had ever done. Powerful jigsaw pieces of an intimate world. Who the man and woman were, he could not guess. They had simply spoken, and he had not censored their words, passionate or estranged. He had worked long hours at these poems, worked harder than he ever had, and although in truth he did not know exactly *what* he had written, he found the poems powerful and mysterious in a way that puzzled him and drew him to his desk as nothing had before.

It was mid-December, the afternoon before the holiday party.

The seminar room darkened quickly, the twilight thickening with the steady fall of freezing rain changing to snow. Miranda wandered into class ten minutes late. She wore a fringed black skirt much shorter than the fashions of the time, black high-heeled boots, and dark green stockings that had the queer, brushed look of suede. Roman watched her legs go by his end of the table and suppressed an impulse to lay his hand against those stockings. He looked away. Someone had passed around a box of candles; the students leaned forward with matches and lighters. From several chairs over, Bernard offered him a paper cup of wine. He accepted it and moved slightly back from the table so that nobody would see his shaking hands. He was angry that this critique would matter so much to him.

Miranda went through several student poems at a brisk pace. Lucy Parry had put up an interesting sonnet; and Shannon Bruno had submitted, to Roman's grudging admiration, another fragmented collage; this time it seemed to be about the fearsomeness of lions. This they discussed without a peep from Miranda—no more lectures on the speciousness of poems based on literary theory. Roman finished his cup of wine and poured himself another. After a short break, halfway through the period, Miranda turned to his work and asked him to read.

Roman began. His voice was loud in his ears, and it seemed to interrupt some atmosphere that had been created in the discussion. He lowered his volume and spoke carefully, keeping his tone flat, so as not to reveal his nerves. Read aloud, to an audience, the poems seemed intimate—almost too intimate. It occurred to him that the class might think he was describing his own experience.

When he had finished, there followed a long pause. Roman glanced surreptitiously around the room, but it was impossible to tell what his classmates were thinking. He wondered if he should clear his throat, to get the conversation going, but decided that it might be seen as a display of emotion. Slowly, trying not to catch anyone's gaze, he took out his notebook.

"Well," somebody said, "these are certainly poems that insist upon being heard."

There was another long pause after that. During this time, Roman wrote in his notebook, "Poems insist on being heard." It was one of his strategies to take notes on everything. He had developed this activity as an undergraduate; it kept him properly employed during the stress of critiques.

"The use of certain words . . . ," someone began, and stopped.

Roman wrote, "Certain words." There were some crude sexual words in the text.

There followed a somewhat halting conversation in which the use of slang words in a formal poem was dissected; the use of those particular slang words, to describe those particular actions, was critiqued.

Roman stole a glance at Phebe Platz. Phebe wore a low-cut green sweater; she sat with her arms folded and her lips pursed. She had chosen the exact middle of the long table, and from his usual spot at the end, Roman observed her frustration with the discussion so far. He was watching for a certain expression he had seen many times during their brief relationship: a smug, preening look when she felt that any event or person reinforced her own opinions or experiences. He knew now, by the absence of this look, that the discussion was not yet punishing enough.

As if she, too, had noticed Phebe, Marlene, one of the other acolytes, cleared her throat. Marlene was a tall, wealthy girl from California with a large nose and a collection of Bakelite bracelets she wore on her long, thin wrists.

"It's my opinion that the use of certain words evinces a want of character," she said.

Roman wrote down, "evinces," and waited, his pen over the page. Surely someone would point out the pointlessness, the utter stupidity of this remark. But no one did.

Then Phebe lifted her face into the candlelight and spoke.

She said, in a loud voice, "I found the use of sex in the poems to be aggressive."

Roman wrote, "Sex aggressive."

Marlene's bracelets clicked together. She asked Phebe what did she mean.

"I mean that the work itself is violent, and aggressive toward the reader."

Roman wrote, "Toward reader."

After a brief pause, Marlene asked, "Do you mean—sexual aggression?"

"As a reader," Phebe said, "I felt that I was being violated."

Roman began, "Phebe feels," and stopped. He would not take notes on this.

To his dismay, no one contradicted her. Instead they spoke for almost twenty minutes about the various sexual acts alluded to, and the language in which they were alluded to, and which passages were most like violation.

Roman glanced at the other men in the class. Bob Lu, to his left, was doodling on the manuscript, and Charlie Krueger's face was hidden. Roman looked at Bernard. Even in the candlelight, he could see Bernard blushing. Bernard could be of no help here. Roman strained to see Miranda. Miranda's curly hair was escaping its knot. She sat very straight, raising her face high above the candles. She wore the faintest smile on her lips.

Mimi Wong, a friend of Phebe and Marlene's, asked, "If a sexual act is alluded to in such crude terms, would one not, as the writer, be subjecting the reader to a form of violence that is, although not physically violent, a form of rape?"

"*Form* of rape?" said Marlene. "Rape is rape. The use of words for the purpose of sexual violence is simply more insidious."

"And yet, equally invidious," Mimi agreed.

There followed a pause. Phebe did not say another word,

but there appeared a trace of the preening expression Roman remembered. It was intolerable. Roman focused all of his strength on seeing indifferent. As he held himself as motionless as possible, a twinge of pain deepened and moved down across his shoulder blades, into his lower back.

Then, from somewhere on the other side of the table, a woman spoke. "I feel compelled to point out . . . ," she began. Roman could not identify the voice, because she spoke so coolly and precisely, as if she, too, found the scene intolerable.

"Although the work might be offensive to some," she began again, "I feel that in focusing on the sexual content of the poems, we are missing some rewarding avenues of discussion."

Roman squinted into the gloom. It was Lucy Parry, looking earnest and particularly pretty.

"Specifically," Lucy said, "I'd like to talk about the lineation. The opening of the second poem, before the dialogue begins, employs line breaks to create a very different tone from the body of the poem. I found myself wondering at this break in tone, and was interested to know if anyone else would have any thoughts on it."

No one spoke. After a moment, Lucy continued. Roman was overwhelmed with gratitude. Lucy was the youngest poet in the program, barely twenty-one, but she had made a serious study of technique. As she spoke, Roman had the opportunity to admire her for her clarity, her intelligence, and her seriousness.

Lucy's remarks were followed by a respectful silence.

Then, Marlene began the conversation again. Exactly what might constitute the rape of a reader? Was it an abuse of artistic power for the poet to rape the reader?

"What do you think?" someone finally asked Miranda, and eleven faces turned toward Miranda's end of the table.

She sat with lowered gaze. Roman could not tell if she had heard. Then, like a mermaid perched upon a rock, she brought both hands to her hair and slowly knotted it behind her. She raised her face into the light: features perfectly balanced, inscrutable.

"In most love poems," she said, "there is some clarity on the question: 'Who is speaking?' Is he, or she, the one who desires? Or the object of desire? In these poems, I find very little desire to speak of."

Was she looking at Roman? She was not. He hated her. He felt with certainty that her aloofness was meant particularly for him. She had ignored him all semester and it could not be entirely his fault.

She continued, still not looking at him, "Who would one rather be? The one who desires, or the object of desire? One's answer to this question might determine if he is meant to be a poet or something else entirely."

"Who wouldn't want to be the object of desire?" asked Phebe.

"'If unequal affections must there be, let the more loving one be me,'" quoted Bernard, looking ahead as if the line had come to him in a dream.

"Meant to be what?" someone asked. "If not a poet, then what is one meant to be?"

"A senator," Miranda said. "A military officer. A playboy." Her gaze flickered in Roman's direction. "No one in the world is thanking you for being a poet." Then she shrugged. There was a world of dismissiveness in her shrug. She peered at her watch. "Time's up."

She buried herself in a leather-bound appointment book. One elegant hand emerged and gestured toward the door, as if to say, Shoo. They had gone ten minutes over the period.

After a brief silence, the students pushed back their chairs. They fumbled for their overcoats, umbrellas, and cigarettes, and ambled out into the freezing rain.

Roman stayed in his seat, splintering with anger.

He felt compelled to wait until even Bernard had gone. Miranda still sat at the other end of the empty table in the flickering reddish light, looking absently through her appointment book.

Roman leaned forward and blew out a candle. Now she seemed to be searching for a pen she had earlier used to secure her knot of hair.

Roman blew out another candle. Soon she would be sitting entirely in the dark. She would be forced to look up, to acknowledge him, if only to ask him to turn on the light. He threw out the stained paper cups and arranged the extinguished candles in their cardboard tray. When he had worked his way up to her end of the table, he paused before the single remaining light.

He cleared his throat.

"Yes?"

"It's me," he said.

"Of course, yes," she said.

"It's Roman," he said, and handed her a pen.

"Thank you, Roman." Her brief glance was a reluctant one.

"Professor Sturgis," he said, "may I ask you a question?"

She nodded at her appointment book.

"Did you like my poems?"

She answered absently, "They're very strong poems."

"Did you *like* them?"

Miranda set down the pen. He had noticed in class her tendency to stare ahead when she was thinking. Now she gazed forward and a chisel line deepened between her eyebrows. "No," she said, and her rich, fluid voice was blunt. "To tell the truth, I did *not* like your poems."

"Go on," he said, shifting his weight.

"If you want me to be honest, you're quite talented," she said. "There's a great deal of power in your work. But there's something hidden about the poems. They draw attention and give nothing back."

She turned again to her appointment book. She was still waiting for him to leave the room. When he did not leave, she made the same shooing gesture she had made to the rest of the class.

Roman jammed his hands into his pockets. "I'm not leaving yet," he said.

"I thought that you were, in some ways, just showing off," she said, drawing a line through something in the book. "Now, will you leave?"

"There's more."

In exasperation, she put down the pen and looked right into his face. He found that he could scarcely meet her eyes. She seemed to recognize not only what he was—one of the many ambitious young men who crowded her after readings and at conferences—but *who* he was—some essence, problematic though it might be, setting him apart from the others. This judgment frightened him and yet it thrilled him, in a way. For there it was again: proof of her capacity for the partiality that he craved.

She was about to speak. Despite his best effort, he turned away, like a man before a firing squad.

"You write as if you have no soul," she said.

There followed the sound of a quick breath, and it was a moment before he understood that the breath was his. He made himself look at Miranda. She was studying the table and he felt viscerally now the sudden cast of reluctance, perhaps regret, that shadowed her features.

"That's not exactly what I meant," she said.

He pressed her. "What *do* you mean?"

"I mean that I don't quite trust your motives for writing poetry."

"Motives?" Certainly, it was a worthy question. How many other things could all of them be doing at that moment, other than arguing and moaning and dissecting and growing more passionate about an activity that mattered to virtually no one and would likely never earn them a living? But why was she saying this to him, Roman? What did his motives matter to her? Was not the power of the poems themselves all that mattered?

"Why do *you* want to write poetry?" he asked. "Why does anyone?"

"Why do we want to fall in love? Why do we want to pray?"

She gazed at him, at once pure and alive, but he stood stunned, unable to reply.

"I mean that these poems are nothing about love," she said.

It was not what he expected. "I wouldn't know," he blurted.

"You wouldn't know." It was a question.

"I've never been in love," he said, suddenly knowing this was true.

Miranda bit her lip. "I'm sorry," she said quietly.

"*I'm* sorry."

His words broke through some gossamer strand of mutual reserve. The air between them thickened. It was a feeling almost palpable, and so was the impression of her floating closer while sitting still, shimmering there in the half-dark as if their very outlines blurred. During the long silence Roman tried to hold her gaze; but, to his vague interest and surprise, she looked away. In the flicker of the candle, her profile was delicate and touched with signs of age, a shadow under the eye, a line curving from the base of her elegant nose to the corner of her mouth. Roman had an unexpected and urgent sense that he was closer—at this very moment—than he had ever been to knowing her: to identifying the uncanny force that guided her. Although he hadn't drunk much in class, he felt as unbalanced as if he had. He reached his hand toward

Miranda's face. Her startled eyes lifted to his, and in his fingertips he felt the throb of his pulse.

Roman withdrew his hand. "Too much wine," he said, and left the room. In the corridor, he could not help glancing back. She sat with her profile lit by the last candle, absolutely still.

EARLY IN ADOLESCENCE, Roman had discovered that he had the capacity to make women violently upset. A brief, bright period of happiness would lead to expectations, then to tears, blaming, and a long, miserable comet's tail of accusations. He would vow to remain solitary, but eventually succumb to the desire for company, only to be scorched by someone else's disappointment. He had many opportunities, but for some reason—perhaps even *because* of the number of opportunities—the sensation of love had eluded him. Miranda's condolences spoke to a thought he had begun to entertain with some frequency: namely that despite an ability to attract many women, he was in some way deficient; and that he might be, because of this, deficient as a poet.

Phebe Platz was only the most recent case. She had been named for a Shakespearean character, she was the godchild of one of the faculty emeriti, and she smoked clove cigarettes, a few things he had found interesting for two weeks of their relationship, before he grew annoyed with the odor of her breath mints and with the way she always sat near the front when they attended readings, looking furtively over her shoulder to see if anyone had noticed them together.

Roman also wearied of Phebe's intimate knowledge of the School faculty. Her godfather, John Weatherby, had fallen in love with a student years before. He had been rejected and was now, according to Phebe, "a shadow of himself." Phebe called Weatherby a saint compared to Thomas Jonquil, an extremely influential, radical poet and frequent adjunct to the program, who slept with a different young male student each time he came to visit. These young men, Phebe said, had all gone on to do quite well. Roman wanted to cover his ears. When he expressed his distaste, Phebe insisted that professors were intimate with students all the time. "It's not illegal," she said, "and if you erased every professor who'd slept with a student, or married a former student, the academy would cease to reproduce."

And yet it was Phebe who had introduced him to Miranda's work, lending him a copy of her first book, *Flight*. Roman had come to the School for its institutional reputation; he had, in honesty, overlooked most of Miranda's work. He was entirely unprepared for *Flight*. There he discovered all of the passion and cruel truth, the fierceness and disdain for the ordinary, that he had failed to find in the relationship with Phebe. Annoyed by his admiration, she picked a quarrel with him for not returning the book. One memorable Sunday night, he ignored her phone calls, then ignored her knocking and shouting from the stairs outside his apartment, while he sat at his desk inside rereading each poem in the collection. On Monday evening, when they broke up, she made him hand it over.

He had wondered, then and since, what this poet, who had written *Flight*, would make of him—of his work, himself. Now he knew.

He wanted to get drunk. Instead of going to the holiday party, which was being held at a bar, he bought a bottle of cheap bourbon and sat in his apartment, pouring shots into a coffee mug and rereading his poems. He read them aloud, over and over, attempting to make his own voice reassert itself over the absurd cacophony of the evening. He would *not* be put off course by the remarks of idiots; he would *not* question himself; he would *not* defend his motives for writing poetry. He worked his way down to the label of the bottle and then, thinking it over, put the bourbon away for later. It was eleven o'clock. Roman stood up and found his balance. He changed his shirt, shaved carefully so as to not nick himself, and got into his car.

He didn't want to go to the party, but there was nothing else to do.

The party was being held in the upstairs room of a ratty local pub. It was not a large room, and nearly all sixty students in the program had already arrived. Roman stood in the doorway, feeling overheated and uncomfortable. The acolytes, in their dramatic makeup and revealing holiday dresses, seemed to him a gauntlet between him and the bar. He held his ground near the door. There he was soon joined by Charlie Krueger, who launched into a witticism about Phebe. Roman awkwardly excused himself, bypassed the acolytes, and ordered a bourbon.

He would wait for Bernard. Bernard had mentioned that,

for this festive occasion, he would alter his routine and stay up late enough to attend the party.

Roman was looking around, trying to discern if Bernard had already been and gone, or where he might otherwise be, when to his surprise, one of the visiting faculty appeared in the doorway and, following him, Miranda Sturgis. None of the faculty typically attended student parties. Miranda wore a simple black coat with its collar turned up against the cold, avoiding the fashion of many scarves affected by her students. Despite her high heels, she seemed shorter than usual, and out of place. He watched her and the visitor, Jonathan Sessions from the Iowa program, enter the room, assess the space, and point to a table past the bar, near the small dance floor. The buzz generated by their appearance was considerable. Miranda made her way to the far corner, near Roman's end of the bar, and removed her coat; she stood in a scarlet dress, revealing a body more frail, more carefully made, than Roman had imagined. He felt, again, the urgency that had surprised him after class. He turned and bought another bourbon.

Someone turned up the music encouragingly, although no one moved out to the floor. Minutes passed, and another song began. Holding on to his bourbon, Roman walked over to Miranda.

"Would you care to dance?"

She squinted up at him, as if attempting to identify him in the dim light. "I'm sorry," she said, reaching for her purse, "I have to use the bathroom."

"Later then." He went back to the bar.

She was gone from the room for quite some time. When she returned, she gave the bar a wide berth.

Roman finished his drink and ordered another. He was running out of cash. But he was appalled by what he had just done. He hated Miranda, and she hated him. He loved her poetry, and she hated his. He had never before possessed the slightest hint of self-destructiveness, had never desired, in the least, personal humiliation, and yet he had embarrassed himself with her twice in the space of a few hours.

"Hello, Roman," someone said.

It was Lucy Parry, looking elegant in a black dress whose plainness, Roman knew from his years at the bank, was really very expensive.

"May I get you a drink?" he asked.

"Sure," she said. He felt foolish, since he had now only a few dollars. It would never occur to Lucy to pay him back. But when he turned to hand her the wine, she reached into her small black bag—even the bag looked expensive—and took out her wallet.

"No," he said, feeling even more foolish. He wanted to give her something. "I owe you at least this much for defending me in class."

"Don't mention it," Lucy said. "They might have been offensive poems, but they were very strong poems." She nodded and smiled as she spoke. She was a slender girl with shining chestnut hair, beautifully shaped, full lips, and appealing shadows under her hazel-green eyes.

He was unable to return her smile. Glancing across the room, he saw Miranda take the dance floor with a male student—a mediocre poet. He refused to watch the dancing and instead stood with Lucy discussing the reading for a literature course. She took her classes seriously.

Roman did his best to say something interesting about Elizabeth Bishop, but what he wanted to ask Lucy was, Did *she* think his poems were offensive? In what way? How was it possible to write honestly about sex without offending somebody? But that conversation seemed at once too intense, too self-centered, and too suggestive.

Stealing an occasional glimpse, he saw two more students approach Miranda. She danced with each of them. The visiting instructor fended off another student and took his turn. Then, during a break in the music, Bernard appeared. Roman had not seen him enter the room. Dressed in his usual sweater and red tie, he walked up to Miranda and made an awkward little bow.

"Roman, look! Bernard is asking Miranda to dance." Lucy, laughing, touched his arm and pointed, forcing Roman to stop pretending that he was not watching them. Bernard stood opposite Miranda, waiting for the next song. "Isn't that sweet?"

Roman nodded. Miranda's hair had slipped halfway from its knot. Her eyes were gleaming.

"Would you like to dance?" Lucy gestured toward the others.

Roman shook his head.

"How are you and Max?" he asked. Max Zabor was a fiercely gifted and erratic writer, a recent graduate of the School who had already made some success as a playwright.

54 LAN SAMANTHA CHANG

"We're off, at the moment," Lucy said.

A dancer touched the flashing strobe. A speck of light flew over Lucy's features, and in that glimpse he thought she looked stricken. He waited to hear more, but she merely held her shoulders still, then released a breath.

They continued to watch the dance together, although it now seemed to him that her black dress was too cautious and her affection pitiful. Yet he considered her worth pursuing. This might be the time, for they would not be in class together for much longer. Also he was feeling lonely. But Lucy was his friend. Somehow, despite her ties to the acolytes, she had reserved the right to enjoy the company of their archenemy, himself, as well as that of the misfit Bernard. She was a gifted poet; she was intelligent and discerning; yet his pleasure in the friendship was possibly too valuable to risk its inevitable ruination.

He let the moment pass. Now Miranda was dancing the jitterbug with Bernard, her movements very straight and light, absolutely carefree, somehow more free and youthful than any of them who were burdened by hopes and expectations. At first Bernard was serious, concentrating on his steps, but as he began to loosen up and make mistakes, which Miranda seemed to love, the two of them became even more fun to watch. The other couples on the floor moved aside. "One more!" cried Bernard, whose traitorous blush now went all the way into his shirt collar. Soon after they began again, he tipped Miranda back into an irretrievable position near a bowl of punch. Her gasping throat and shoulders glittered in the rented strobe light. Roman saw Lucy glance at him.

He turned to the bar again, to hide the desire that must have shone in his face.

Later, he drove slowly in an effort to control his drunkenness. It was a crisp winter night. The streets were covered with snow, and there was a stillness in the air that foretold more. Everyone knew where Miranda lived, in the same way everyone knew that she was married, had been married since she was twenty-four, first to Dane Bonham, a man fifteen years older than she and an influential literary critic at Berkeley; and now to a Baltimore architect named Michael Howe. She saw Michael two weekends a month and they spent their summers in London. Miranda was forty-six. There were no children.

The house stood on the edge of a good neighborhood, near a maze of smaller streets, where he could park his car and wander, unnoticed, into the alley behind. It was a spacious Victorian, with a porch that wrapped around two sides—far too large for a childless, commuting couple. The outside was painted beige, with dark red and green trim that in the night looked black. Half-covered rabbit tracks crisscrossed the yard. The barren spines that remained in her untidy gardens were bent with snow. Roman made an effort to walk carefully, but he stumbled after unlatching the gate; a bit of snow fell into his eyes as he slipped under the trellis. He stopped to wipe his face. For a moment, he stood sniffing the winter air, the mixture of burning firewood and cold, which had spoken to him since childhood of other people's easy lives. Even at night, in the dark, Miranda's house said careless safety, it said comfort.

High in an upstairs corner of the house, a dim light shone.

Roman stepped onto the back porch. "Miranda," he shouted.

There was no answer.

"Miranda, Miranda." His baritone, in which he took some pride, ricocheted up off the porch and toward her window.

There was no response. Still, she did not turn out the light.

He began to sing.

> *"An owl and a pussycat went to sea,*
> *In a beautiful pea-green boat.*
> *They took some honey, and plenty of money,*
> *Wrapped up in a five-pound note."*

He imagined her upstairs with her book, frowning at the text, as if by fervent reading she could will him gone.

> *"O lovely Pussy! O lovely Pussy!*
> *What a beautiful Pussy you are,*
> > *You are,*
> > *You are!*
> *What a beautiful Pussy you are!"*

Still, there was no response.

"Miranda," he shouted, "come down, or I will next recite a series of my poems."

The wind picked up as if the house itself had sighed in irritation. After a long pause, he heard footsteps on the stairs.

The door opened and she peered out. "Roman," she said.

She wore a white robe that was too large for her. He felt torn between excitement and resentment that she had such confidence, and so little fear of him, that she had come downstairs, and he looked coldly at the rough tie around her waist and at her breasts half visible in the deep V.

"Roman," she said, "you're drunk."

"I am."

"What do you want?"

"I need help," he told her. "With my poems."

She reached for her robe and pulled it more closely around her body. When she spoke, her tone was stern. "My office hours are on Wednesdays. You haven't come to office hours all semester."

"I'm not one of your sniveling acolytes, you mean."

"Spare me the petty social politics of your sex life."

He had not expected that she would notice any of that. "I'm your student," he said stiffly. "I'm entitled to your attention."

For a long moment she scrutinized his face. "You haven't come to office hours all semester," she repeated. Then she peered down at her slippers.

Watching her intently now, Roman focused on the dark fringes of her eyelashes.

She went on slowly, speaking almost to herself. "You sit in class," she said, "glowering at everyone who speaks and saying almost nothing. You don't show us a single poem for fourteen weeks. Then, in week fifteen, after the last class, you show up stone drunk at my door at two-thirty a.m. and say that you want help."

"Need help," he corrected her.

She said, in a lower voice, "Need help."

Roman moved closer to her, to her house. "You don't like my poems," he said. "I know you don't. But I do have a soul, and you know that, too. No one—not even you—has the privilege to say what you did."

When she did not reply, he knew that he had spoken the truth. He had nothing more to do but wait for her to make up her mind. She stood silently on the threshold with a bar of pale light across her throat and shoulders. Then she opened wide the door and led him into the house.

ROMAN DID NOT GO home to Massachusetts over winter break. He had important fellowship deadlines coming up, he told his grandmother, applications that required his utmost concentration. This was largely true.

He bent his will upon the poems. It was hard work. He had never felt so humbled by words. He had never dreaded words as much as he did in those weeks. Words stalked him: words ambushed his mind in the middle of the night; words jumped out of newspapers and theater marquees and other people's poems. Still, he worked. The critique had hurt his confidence in a way he tried not to think about; but he now had a deadline to drive him, and, as Miranda told him again and again: in the face of a deadline, there is no need for confidence.

If he had thought that getting Miranda's personal attention would be a way of gaining her praise, he was mistaken. She was as critical a reader as she had ever been, insisting upon revisions and then questioning every word of them. But she had let him know, implicitly, that he was worth her attention, and he struggled to write well enough that the two of them would not be proven false.

"What I think I see," she told him once, "is that there's something real beneath the sex and anger in these poems—a sense of almost elemental loneliness. It's buried somewhere in these voices, and it needs to be brought out."

From Christmas Eve until New Year's Eve, every day it snowed. Each morning he brewed a pot of coffee and brought it to his desk. He read and worked and reread, drinking the coffee black and pacing in a small circle near the window until late afternoon, when he quit in misery and disgust, anxiety jangling. At this point, he would jam his hat over his ears and jog over to the gym, or to see Bernard—who did not have a telephone—to urge his friend along to Oscar's, where a few other students who had stayed in town might be hunched at the bar, watching football players scrambling in snow. After a reasonable dinner hour, or what he imagined would be dinner hour for Miranda, he would make his way to her house, the latest versions of his poems in his pocket.

It was not a spoken arrangement. He didn't even know for sure why she was in town. She'd once remarked—or so the acolytes said—that marriage, in its everyday practice, was exhausting, and that Michael's job in Baltimore provided essential time for work. Roman knew that Michael had partial custody of a child from his first wife; he was probably spending the holidays with this child. Roman saw Miranda every night, including Christmas and New Year's Eve, which they spent in bed without mentioning the occasions. Miranda was presumably above such petty conventions. Roman kept silent as an instinctive variation of a strategy he had developed over the years to avoid whatever woman with whom he was involved on major holidays.

After all, there was no sense in their involvement, and no future. He assumed that their relationship would end when he completed the revisions for his fellowship applications. After the deadline, which was January 15, he would have no more excuses to stop by. He was enrolled in another seminar for his final semester and would not see her in class. There would be no hard feelings, and they would nod at each other in the hallway or at a reading.

In the meantime, he pelted her with questions. Although she retained, even in lovemaking, a certain privacy, he found her curiously approachable now that he saw her only at home. Her manner at the School was indeed a screen she placed between herself and her students. Behind that screen, she was a regular person like everyone else—or, Roman believed, perhaps a little more memorable than everyone else. What they did in bed together, though not new to him, lingered in his thoughts, and he sometimes found it difficult to return to his own life.

Early one morning, as he prepared to leave, she sat cross-legged on the unmade bed in white pajamas. She was threading a cord back into the small mesh bag in which she washed her stockings.

Roman stood in his socks, dreading the return to his unfinished poems. He found it maddening and comforting: her habit of tending to small household details in his presence. He watched her tie the cord onto a tiny safety pin, squinting slightly over the little knot. She pushed the safety pin into the hem of the bag. Her hands were graceful and precise. He could see that she took pleasure in her task, a kind of pleasure she did not bring to class.

"Why do you hate Shannon's work so much?" he asked.

"I don't hate Shannon's work." Her voice was low and pleasant. "As a matter of fact, I lobbied against the other faculty to admit her to the School. And I think she's done some decent work here. There was a poem she wrote last year, also about confinement."

"I didn't know you took her seriously."

"Why wouldn't I?" Her hands paused. The faint line deepened between her brows, but he knew her well enough now to see that she wasn't angry, only thinking.

"Ah, you're remembering the class," she said. "If Shannon is to be a true poet of the kind she wishes to be—a true poet of the avant-garde—she will get over it." Roman listened more closely. "If my reaction stops her, then something else would have stopped her just the same. Too many rejection letters. A bad review."

She removed the safety pin, knotted the ends of the small cord together, and pulled them tight. She often stopped speaking just as he'd begun to listen most hungrily. She seemed to believe that worldly success was a misfortune, and that her instruction for attaining success would be dangerous to him. As if he were a fragile youth, entrusted to her guidance.

As Roman bent down to lace his shoes, she spoke again.

"It's not an easy life," she said. "No one is dispensing favors." She slid her gaze toward him, smiling. "Excepting yours truly."

He could not help smiling in return.

On January 15, he said goodbye to Miranda with more than the usual care. He thanked her for helping him finish his applications. It was almost noon when he left her. As he made his way out the back gate, he glanced once more at the house and saw her there in the window, watching him.

His hands shook as he turned his applications over to the postal clerk. He stepped out of the post office and wandered, empty-handed now, staring into store windows, or up at the sky, a dark, uncluttered gray but for stark tree branches and cawing crows. For the length of several minutes, the world held still, perfect in the knowledge that a burden had been released.

Slowly, aimlessly, Roman made his way toward his car. He stopped in at Oscar's. Hours passed, and it was very late when he left the pub. He turned down a side street that led toward a small, dark square. Here, Bernard had told him, lay the origins of Bonneville: a hushed, leafless cemetery and two stone churches. He meandered through the shadowy plot and recognized the marker of the city patriarch: an imposing granite rectangle half buried in snow.

He was not in love with Miranda. Of this much, he was certain. He could not be in love with her because he had no expectations.

And he assumed she was not in love with him. She was married, after all. She never took off her ring.

If he was not in love with her, nor she with him, was there, in fact, any harm in continuing the affair? He brushed the snow from a granite cross. It would be impolite to break things off abruptly.

He drove across town, taking care as usual to park in a neighborhood where someone who might recognize his car would not guess whom he had come to visit.

As he traced a new, elaborate route from his parking spot to Miranda's back alley, he felt his lungs free up, expanding with each breath. There were so many possibilities, so many other lives. He imagined a kinship with each living thing: with the dogs who spilled their notes into the frosty air; with the bats huddled into the eaves of toolsheds and carriage houses; with the murmuring cicadas asleep belowground. Was this the way Miranda felt? Was it this she'd felt when she was dancing, when she wrote her poems?

She had shown him the spare key tucked under the eave; he let himself into the house and let his eyes adjust to the dim light. He tiptoed up the stairs, remembering with sudden longing her large, soft bed surrounded by a nest of books and papers. The door was ajar; he pushed it softly open.

IN THE MEANTIME, at the School, things went on as usual. The students were still enamored of and terrified by Miranda. In the evenings, at Oscar's, they discussed the latest bludgeonings and studied the constellation of rumors surrounding her. That Miranda had been forbidden to teach undergraduates after flunking an entire class. That Miranda had persuaded the School to pay the rent on her sabbatical Paris pied-à-terre. That Miranda had once been involved with Berryman, whose poem "Homage to Mistress Bradstreet" had been in truth about Miranda. No one pointed out that if this were the case, she would have been a child at the time.

Listening to their remarks, refusing to contribute, unwilling even to look at anyone, was curiously pleasurable. Roman had never before known so viscerally the power and comfort of a secret. None of them had seen the square of moonlight on her bedroom floor. None of them knew that she loved cheap milk chocolate, or that she wore high heels because she thought she was too short. Along with this, there was the pleasure of thinking about the time they had spent together. He alone had tasted the depth of her generosity, and it fattened him to hear his classmates hash out its dregs.

On such an evening, Roman extricated himself from a larger group to join Bernard and Lucy. They sat in a comfortable, roomy, dark old booth, its table scarred with ancient social history. Bernard had no quarrel with drinking beer. After the three of them had ordered a second pitcher, he sat back, red-faced and happy, in his corner of the booth. He took off his glasses, folded them, and rubbed his eyes.

"I've been thinking," he said, "about our conversation last semester. Following Shannon's—"

"—bludgeoning," said Roman.

Lucy laughed, but Bernard seemed not to hear. "I had a few thoughts I tried to express at the time," he went on, "but I did a poor job of it. It seems to me that the old question applies here: 'Can poetry—'"

He was interrupted by a hoot from a neighboring booth, where Bob Lu, Shannon herself, and several of their other classmates were playing a drinking game in which the goal was to compose within ten seconds a limerick about the death of a famous poet.

"Isn't it a little early for this?" asked Lucy, rolling her eyes at Roman in a way he could not help thinking was flirtatious.

Bernard didn't even acknowledge the limerick game. He had always found it disrespectful. "As I was about to say, 'Can poetry be taught?' I believe that no—not in any conventional sense," he continued.

Roman frowned but said nothing.

Lucy ventured, "So you don't think she should even try?"

"I don't. In fact, I wonder if that may do harm. I was thinking about your idea, Roman, that Miranda is indifferent to us. I think it's not important whether she pay us mind. It's most important, I think, that we are aware of *her*, that we spend every opportunity to observe her in the most minute ways possible, for it is she who will show us how to live a life of poetry."

Lucy said, "So what you're saying, Bernard, is that we learn from her no matter what. That she can be indifferent and also a good teacher."

Roman said nothing. There were things he had once wanted to say—would have said. Things he had once believed. That more practical instruction would be of help to them. That she didn't care—didn't even notice—them or their lives. The problem was that she had helped him in ways that were not at all practical, and that he now knew she *did* notice—and, he realized, *did* care. The new riddle was *why* she pretended not to notice and not to care.

The room was slowly filling with the ghosts of poets. At age thirty-eight, Federico García Lorca had been executed during the Spanish Civil War. At age thirty-nine, Dylan Thomas had drunk himself to death with eighteen shots of whiskey. At age forty, Frank O'Hara had been run over by a dune buggy on Fire Island. Also at forty, Edgar Allan Poe had been found delirious on the streets of Baltimore and died shouting a name no one knew.

Bernard was saying, "I think that, on occasion, the idea of teaching changes as we move from a model that is more undergraduate to one of a practitioner, an apprentice—"

The noise erupted once again from the booth.

"Alexander Pushkin!" someone yelled, and it seemed that everyone in the bar was cheering.

Bob Lu stood wavering on his chair, in a cloud of cigarette smoke. An athletic young man with an appealing cowlick, he was widely acknowledged as one of the most promising poets in the first-year class.

"Get your ass on the chair!" shouted the bartender.

Bob squinted his eyes shut and began.

"This poet of great virtuosity
Wed a girl of extreme fructuosity
And when made a cuckold
Unwisely swashbuckled
And died of his own bellicosity!"

The door opened and the poet Thomas Jonquil entered the bar. He was in town to give a reading—someone had picked him up at the airport and had brought him directly to Oscar's. Roman thought with admiration of a Jonquil poem he had read in college. Then he remembered what Phebe had said about Thomas Jonquil, and turned back to his table.

"Bernard," said Lucy gently, "don't you think you're idealizing Miranda in a way? I saw her in the Food Zoo"—this was their nickname for the Bread and Circus market—"arguing with her husband"—Roman dropped his eyes—"because she wanted to buy asparagus." Roman had not known Miranda liked asparagus. "Her husband was saying that it made his piss smell bad, Miranda was saying that he was too fastidious, and that she was going to make him less fastidious—and she French-kissed him"—Bernard winced—"right there in the Food Zoo, at the checkout line."

Roman had seen Michael once, also at the Food Zoo, in the wine aisle last autumn. He had seemed older than Miranda, although Roman had now lost perspective on Miranda's age.

Roman turned to Lucy. "Do you find Michael attractive?"

She gave him a quizzical glance. "I suppose, if you go for éminence grise. But I don't like kissing men with beards."

Roman had no reply to this. Lucy changed the subject to New York City, where she and Bernard were both planning to move after graduation. She had gone to school at Sarah Lawrence and now recounted her weekend forays into Manhattan.

In the next booth, Thomas Jonquil leaned over the table

and whispered something to Bob Lu. Bob informed the group, in limerick form, that Paul Celan had written *départ Paul* in his pocket calendar for the date on which he threw himself into the Seine. Bob seemed flattered by Jonquil's attention, and the players were pleased that the older man had joined the game. Roman felt relieved that he and Miranda kept their own affair a secret. He studied Jonquil's blunt, folded features and wondered why it was he made his romantic forays into the student world so public. What was he teaching? What were they learning? Or was it widely understood that this type of attachment was a rite of passage in the lives of poets, as commonplace as tragic death?

It was the kind of question he wished to ask Miranda, but, thinking it over, he decided it would be better not to bring it up.

GRADUATION WAS A BLACK emptiness that threatened to devour all of the second-year students, but particularly Roman, with his narrow options and high expectations. He vowed not to return to banking and so, without the School, he had nothing. Several of the others, such as Lucy, would receive help from their families: the use of a vacation house; a credit card; a car. Roman had only his hopes and ambitions, a glistening, iridescent shield protecting him from poverty and failure. Before, he had also had his confidence. But now, at unexpected times, this belief grew thin as a tissue and he would feel the emptiness, threatening to swallow him. What if? What if? There were no answers.

He went to see Miranda almost every night, bringing drafts and pieces of his work. He was still listening to the words of his imaginary lovers, developing a sequence of monologues. On each visit, he came to her house convinced that the project should be discarded. But as she went over what he had written, he would feel his anxiety calming, line by line, until he was persuaded it would be possible to keep going.

They kept one unspoken rule from the earliest days of their relationship: that Roman was free to come or go. Miranda never phoned him or insisted that he stay with her. They did not make plans.

He felt this freedom gave him a modicum of power. His other power, he knew, lay in his youth. She seemed to crave it in her very pores. Her craving went beyond an interest in his face or body. The oddest things would trigger it: his muddy boot prints on the stairs; or his statement, made when they were finishing a pizza, that he was still hungry. One of their most memorable nights of lovemaking occurred after he admitted to her that he could not remember the death of President Kennedy.

On a sparkling afternoon in early March, he glimpsed her on the way to campus, severe and elegant in her winter coat and high, narrow boots. They shared a few rare minutes outdoors together, walking between heaps of melting snow. Roman made a snowball. Taking pleasure in her laughter, he showed off like a schoolboy, aiming carefully, making a neat white circle on a telephone pole.

Upon reaching the School, they went to their respective seminars. He sat impatiently as his ran overtime, inwardly fuming at the dull critiques of uninspired poems. When seminar was finally over, he hurried to Miranda's house. She was, as he had hoped, eager to make love.

Afterward, as they lay together, he complained about his class. "I'm absolutely sure," he said, "that I've outgrown it all: the seminar, the seminar system, even the School. But where else can I make progress? I know now that my poems aren't yet right. I'm working harder than I ever have, but I still have so far to go before I reach my goal."

After a silence, Miranda turned to him. "And what is your goal?" she asked.

"Mastery," he blurted, miserably. "To reach a point where I'm certain I've gained artistic mastery."

In the moment that followed, he suspected he had said something ridiculous. But Miranda merely placed a hand on his chest. She looked at him with an expression both acutely pained and faraway. "If I could change a single thing about my life," she said gently, "I would not have been so unhappy when I was young."

FOR SPRING BREAK, she flew to London to spend two weeks with Michael. In a gesture of indifference to the School's academic calendar, she planned to stay abroad for an extra week and not return until classes were already in session.

On the first day of her absence, Roman felt relieved. His own stark room held new appeal, and when he went outdoors, he marveled at the signs of spring. He sat down to write and felt his gift flood back into his hands. But by the end of the week, his words began to seem intransigent and thin, and he urgently wanted to see Miranda.

This feeling—as if he were living in high altitude and any movement might put him out of breath—persisted when he was doing the most ordinary things: getting his hair cut; having tea and oranges at Bernard's while reading over Bernard's latest draft of a letter to a great, declining poet; or standing before his own group of composition students, insisting with vehemence, despite his own wish to remain detached, that they pay attention to the placement of an apostrophe.

He was obliged to reconsider the relationship.

Making love had not made them into equals. There was Miranda's position at the School; and there was Michael, in London—while for Roman there was no one. Although he had no desire to sustain things beyond a certain point, the fact that it was impossible rankled him. It now galled him that she took pleasure in his youth, as if it were childishness. He thought of how she fed him, soothed him, petted him behind closed shades. She treated him with an almost laughable solicitude, worrying about the thickness of his overcoat or whether he liked raw onions, and listening patiently to his complaints about the other students.

In truth, she held the worldly power and he had power over only her desire; that she desired him as she did was her one weakness. And yet—Roman thought—as if depriving him of his single advantage, she did not seem to perceive it as a weakness. She did not hide her desire from him; she only playfully resisted and in the end gave in to every kiss. He had once proposed seducing her after class, with a chair wedged under the doorknob, on the long table littered with wine-stained paper cups and blown-out candles. She did not reject the idea. It was he who held back, out of cowardice and also a queer desire to protect her. He had wondered briefly why she did not show more concern about the risk involved.

Had she reached a point, with Michael, where she no longer valued the marriage enough to care if the affair might be discovered? If this was the case, why had she turned her back on Roman and gone to London?

On the night of her return, Roman went to her house, determined to start a conversation, but she treated him with affection, as if she'd never been away. The following morning, he woke up once again in her bed.

He lay next to her, taking in the details he had missed while she was gone: outside, the dripping icicles; inside, the quiet pleasure of sunlight on the comforter. Miranda wore nothing under her big white robe, a robe he liked, for sentiment's sake, although he was quite certain it belonged to her husband. At some point he noticed that her eyes were fixed on his face. There was again that quality to her gaze he couldn't place, both belonging to and separate from the moment. It was an expression he had not seen on the face of any other woman with whom he'd been involved.

"What are you thinking about?" he asked. The moment he spoke, he was aware of the sophomoric cliché, but Miranda never seemed to notice such things, or perhaps she was accustomed to his asking stupid questions.

"I am imprinting this upon my memory," she said. "The

southern exposure of a winter morning light, the sounds of thaw, water dripping off the eaves, the squirrels."

Roman thought that he would try to make a note in his book. He had a page set aside for the things she had said. "Do you do that often?" he asked. "Remember things?"

She frowned slightly, and the winter light she had mentioned bit into the crease on her forehead. "Yes," she said. "Sometimes I seem to know, in the split second of a moment, that it will be a moment I'll want to keep."

Roman felt a sudden restlessness, glad he was not yet forty-six. He drew a deep breath.

"Miranda," he began, "why didn't you marry a poet?"

She ignored his intention, which had been about the nature of her marriage. "That's a good question," she said thoughtfully, as if they were in class. Then, with a soft laugh, "Male writers are like women. The subtle observation, the complexity. A successful mating between a male and female poet would be like a mating between two unicorns. Nine times out of ten, it's doomed."

"Are you saying male poets should mate with no one? With each other?"

"Of course, the ones who truly like women, like them very much." Her eyes crinkled with amusement as she watched his face. "I'm saying I wouldn't marry a true poet, wouldn't trust a real poet farther than I could throw him."

Roman nodded. She often used the enigmatic phrase "true poet," and he was too self-conscious to ask her to explain.

"And the male poets of our more recent, more enlightened generation?" he asked.

"You?" Had she forgotten he was in the room? But she was smiling directly at him now. "Are you still trying to get me to assess your validity as a poet?"

"No," he said, feeling foolish. "I wasn't." He did not tell her this: that since Miranda had first let him into her house, any commentary about his poems, other than hers, slid away from him.

"What is at the bottom of this persistent series of questions?"

"You," he said, giving in. "You're married. You're supposed to be with your husband. What are you doing with me?"

"Is that important?" She turned her gaze toward the ceiling so that he could not see her face.

Emboldened, he said, "You don't love your husband anymore."

Miranda did not move.

He blurted, "You love me!"

She shrugged. Her robe slipped slightly off her collarbone. From that gesture of feigned indifference, which he recognized from a more public setting, he knew he was right.

This absolute certainty unsettled him. He half hoped that she would continue with a joke. Instead she said, "I'm sorry I went away to see Michael. It was difficult, and I did worry that it might hurt you."

He felt the heat of righteousness. "*I'm* not the one who's married," he said, flushing. "I wondered how this was affecting *you*."

An answering color rose into her cheeks. As Roman

watched with some alarm, she said slowly, "Tell me what you mean."

"I just wondered," he said, "since . . . since you're in a morally compromised position." He waited for her response, but she said nothing, merely waited. The truth began to feel inadequate, and he regretted that he had brought up the subject. "At work. And in your marriage," he pushed on. "As for me—I'm free of those restrictions," he added.

After a moment's pause, she spoke slowly, phrasing her thoughts with care. "I see. Does my situation—bother you?"

"Of course not," he said. "But—" he began, then stopped. He did not know, and he would not have wished to tell her whether it did. He felt a fresh wave of discomfort. "I suppose you wish now you hadn't opened the door for me that night," he said, changing the subject.

"I knew it when I opened the door."

"Then why—"

"Believe me," she said. She was still studying the ceiling. "The minute I saw you, I had a feeling I should walk right back upstairs. But sometimes, a situation arises—feelings arise—and one can't, or shouldn't, choose—"

"What feelings do you mean?"

"I don't know if I could explain them to you, Roman." She closed her eyes, uncharacteristically discouraged, and he felt a pang of fear. Could it be possible that she had no defensible explanation for what she had done? It was as if he were watching her lose her way. He did not like the feeling. "No, let me try," she said. She opened her eyes and turned, gazing at him soberly. "Do you wish to ever marry?"

"Of course," he said. "Of course, I'll get married and have children." He nodded, coupling the distant, and yet certain, desire for marriage with the equally distant, certain prospect that he would someday have a child.

"Well, then, when you do marry, you may discover," she said, "sometimes, even in the most companionable partnerships, there exists—something outside the marriage. Something with its source of heat, its own poetic life, entirely unrelated, off the record. In this case—" She broke off her sentence and stared vividly at nothing, then turned away from him. "It's true, after all," she said, and it seemed to him that she was speaking to herself, "I'm in a bad position."

He could no longer see her face, only her cloud of hair. Threaded through the curls, there were glistening strands of silver. If she *did* think about the risks involved—and Roman let himself consider her job, her reputation, and her marriage to this husband he had never met—

He felt, intensely, and for the first time with her, the impulse toward flight.

"Look," he said, sitting upright, "if the risks are too much for you, I completely understand. I mean, I understand if you want to stop."

She turned back to him slightly, acknowledging his offer with a little smile. "Roman," she said, "there are risks for you as well."

"Sure," he said, automatically.

She paused. "Risks as a person, and, as a poet."

He frowned. "What do you mean?"

"Roman—"

In her deep intake of breath, he heard weariness and strain. Yet now he could also read, in her reluctance to speak, a determination to get at the truth. It was a determination he had first glimpsed in class, and that he now dimly sensed to be some kind of burden for her.

"Don't tell me!" he exclaimed. "I don't want to know!"

His panicked voice filled the room. She held still for a moment. Then she shrugged, and when she spoke, it was with an effort at insouciance. "All right," she said. "What I meant to say, before, is that our relationship isn't related to any of your ways of thinking. It's a different thing entirely."

"What is it?"

She smiled at him again, in a faint echo of that marvelously reassuring and self-absorbed way she had in class. "Let's say that this is part of your poetic education."

He turned, suddenly hurt.

"Roman," she said. She reached over and put her hand beneath his chin, guiding him to her. He did not want her to see his face. He pulled the robe down off her shoulders and reached for her.

After that, Roman tried to let things between them cool off a little, although he was not able to stay away for more than a few nights. During that time, he made an effort to focus on his poems. He tried to forget about their disturbing conversation—for whenever it entered his mind, he had the hollow and regretful feeling that he had failed some kind of test.

———

HE RECEIVED THE LETTER on a cold day in early April. He was one of four selected from more than three hundred applicants to receive a fellowship for emerging poets at a university in California. He would receive a stipend, health benefits, and a summer allowance, as well as the opportunity to work as a paid teaching assistant for a senior professor.

As Roman stood before his mailbox on that cold, cloudy morning, he had a sense of the future opening before him, pouring out the dazzling pale gold light and the perpetual mild weather of California.

That evening he did not go to the gym or the bar, but headed uninvited, much earlier than usual, to Miranda's house. Now was the time to tell her. His heart thumped with an emotion close to fear, the physical knowledge that something was about to change.

The poems he had revised under her tutelage had won him passage away from her. He imagined she would think this irony both peculiar and right.

But the sight of her at the door, absently smiling in her reading glasses, stopped him. It might have been the familiar pencil tucked behind her ear, or the curl escaping from her pinned-up hair. Whatever the reason, he felt confused, and he could not bring himself to tell her. She was in a serious mood, what he privately called her "teachery" frame of mind. An invisible force field of intellect surrounded her. A fat, dog-eared anthology lay open on the couch. He suspected she had meant to spend the evening preparing for class.

Roman turned over the book. She was reading "For My Daughter."

"Weldon Kees?" Roman asked, surprised. "What a sourpuss."

Miranda said, "'I have no daughter. I desire none.' That sonnet is a gorgeous piece of work."

He wanted to protest. He had sometimes wondered why Miranda had no children, but thought it better not to ask.

Knowing he should leave, he sat down sullenly on the couch. When she began to discuss the text, he found it difficult to concentrate, but the sound of her voice was comforting. He recalled that Kees had suffered from depression all of his life. In 1955, when he was forty, he had parked his car near the Golden Gate Bridge and disappeared.

"Roman," said Miranda, "do you ever write about your mother?"

He had told her about his mother, once, in the middle of the night.

"You should try to do it sometime, Roman."

"Okay," he said, certain he would not. He reached for the daydream about his mother that he had begun inventing as a child and had perfected in college. Someday, years from now, when he was older and a great poet, his mother would hear of him and find him.

Unhappy and confused, he leaned against Miranda's shoulder. When could he tell her about his news? She opened the book at a wider angle and kept reading aloud, but he had broken her instructive mood and heard, after a moment, solicitude steal into her voice. He pressed his cheek against her sweater. The smell of her perfume was stronger there. He could almost believe he had not yet received the letter. Of course, the letter was still his—he wanted nothing more— but he had not yet received it, he was innocent. He deserved this innocence, for now.

"Roman," she said, stroking his hair, "are you there?" He relaxed into her arms, feigning sleep. "Roman," she whispered, and he said nothing. She caressed even more gently, feather strokes over his forehead, then along his eyebrows and finally his closed lids. "The owl and the pussycat went to sea," she murmured, her breath close to his ear, "in a beautiful pea-green boat. They took some honey, and plenty of money, wrapped up in a five-pound note." Warmth and drowsiness flowed into his veins. It was a feeling more delicious than he had thought possible. He fought against the waves of real sleep that threatened to close over him, first gaining a little and then sinking. Some time had passed but still she touched his face and murmured words he had lost the need to understand. There was something he had to tell her, something of importance, but although he parted his lips to speak, he could not move them. He felt a light kiss on his temple and dropped straight into sleep.

ON THE FINAL DAY of the semester, the director of the School held a graduation party. It was a brilliant day after a rain, the city rinsed cool under a blue sky scudding with tiny clouds. The students brought their families. Roman had no family but Emily, who had been unable to leave the house in Massa-chusetts. But Miranda would be there.

He arrived a half hour later than promised. He had to sell his aging car—it would not make the trip to California—and before he dropped it off, he needed to deliver some furniture to an incoming student. He was flying to San Francisco in a week, and had gotten rid of almost all of his possessions. His books would be shipped by UPS—including Miranda's grad-uation gift, an inscribed copy of *Flight*. He had taken the gift back to his apartment, glanced at the inscription, and placed it nervously into a box.

Packing, weighing, and measuring the boxes was a wel-come distraction from his anxiety over the prospect of telling Miranda about his plans to move. His reluctance to disclose his news had developed into a secret, with all the compli-cations and fears of secrecy. The simplest part had been concealment—to hide his preparations to leave town from Miranda and from everyone. When Lucy and Bernard asked about his plans, he feigned indecision, hinting that he might move closer to his grandmother. He told Miranda that he might stay in town and pick up a composition course.

But each time they made love, he felt a queer evanescence, as if her body were slipping from his grasp. He would hold her more tightly and make love to her more fervently. When he felt sorry for the dishonesty, he reminded himself of their unspoken rule: that he was free to come and go. It was, and it had always been, his power in the relationship.

Yes, he was free to come and go. As he parked his bicycle,

stood back, and took in the sparkling air, it seemed that the whole world lay before him and there was nothing to feel bad about. He could even look fondly upon the acolytes, who were now scattered before him on the lawn, in groups and with their parents, their colorful summer dresses revealing their slender arms.

"You're here right in time for the group photo," someone told him happily. It was Lucy. He followed her across the lawn to where everyone was assembling and where, he was quite glad to see, Miranda waited, in a white dress and ridiculously high-heeled white sandals. She was tall enough to join him in the back row, and they held hands, hidden by the group. There were toasts and balloons and multiple photographs taken by many cameras. The group wandered apart and he realized, with a sudden, faint pressure of regret, that they would never be together again.

Lucy introduced Roman to her parents, Ned and Sophie. They were well dressed, slim, and proud of her. She invited him to dinner with them and, feeling like an orphan, he refused. He was unprepared for the dilution of his friends by family. Even Bernard had a tall, stern aunt Anne, who had taken the bus out from Chicago.

He searched the lawn for Miranda's white dress and found her by the flower beds, surrounded by students and their parents. He broke through the crowd with glasses of champagne. "I've already had two," she protested, but she took the plastic flute and toasted him. Her eyes sparkled with pride. "To your success, dear Roman." He was suddenly near tears. "Roman has written a stunning thesis," Miranda told somebody's grandmother. Roman tried to smile. Miranda gave him a penetrating glance over her champagne and excused herself to the group. She drifted into the empty house. A minute later, he followed.

Behind her on the stairs, he watched her sway on her high heels; and once they were together inside one of the rooms, she giggled tipsily at the dozens of stuffed animals that watched them from the narrow bed. Roman locked the door. The child, he knew, was already on vacation in New Hampshire, with her mother. Muffling Miranda's shrieks of laughter, he silently pushed her down among the animals and pulled the straps of her dress down over her shoulders.

"No words today, Roman?" she asked.

He said nothing. He sensed keenly now that even as he held her, she was somehow passing from existence.

"Watch out," she murmured, "I'm your professor."

"Not anymore. Hold still," he said.

She smiled into his arm. It was a solace to make this final struggle with her, to wordlessly, laughingly bring her to yield what she pretended to withhold from him.

When they finished she lay drowsily against the rumpled spread, watching him button his shirt. They had been inside for more than half an hour, and Roman thought their mutual absence from the party might be noticed. He put on his trousers, socks, and shoes. He reached for her underwear on the bright carpet and handed it to her. Then, after she had gotten dressed and he had finished smoothing and tucking in the child's bedspread of blue sky and white clouds, he drew one last, tight breath, and spoke.

"I got an Argent Fellowship," he said. "In California."

She was pulling back her hair. He watched her upraised arms, her graceful wrists as she finished twisting her curls back into their knot. Then she sat down on the bed. So she had not been expecting this. He looked nervously around the room for something to do.

"Have you accepted it?" she asked.

Roman was on his hands and knees, gathering stuffed animals. "I'm flying out end of next week," he said.

For a moment, she did not respond. Then she drew her knees together and turned her face away from him. He felt distressed somehow that she did not wish him to see.

He said, stupidly, "You're the first person I've told," and, after a pause, was relieved to hear her reply. "Congratulations, Roman dear." Her voice shook in an effort to control her confusion.

He wanted her to say that he deserved his fortune, what a good fellowship it was. But she sat without a word, her hands laced tightly on her knees. Roman stood awkwardly, knowing it would be wrong to go, but wishing he could leave.

"Do you—" She took another shaking breath. "Do you need someone to take you to the airport?"

"Bob Lu can do it," he said, "If you drive me, someone might see us there together."

"I see," she said. "I see, now, how you want it to be."

She would not look at him. She was, indeed, angry, but she would not give him relief by taking her anger out on him. Roman felt miserable at the familiar sight of the lines on her neck, the slight looseness to the skin at the base of her jaw.

"I'm indebted to you," he said, somewhat unsteadily. She had let him into her house when he had told her what he needed. He wondered if in all of her care and concern she had ever recognized that what he might need most, at some point, was to make his own way. He had always assumed that their intimacy, with its own extravagances and private jokes, must come to an end. It had flourished behind walls and must someday seal itself off completely. Surely she must have known this as well.

He would not think about it now. "Well," he said, tucking in his shirt, "I guess one of us should go downstairs first."

Minutes later, standing with Lucy in the middle of the green, green lawn littered with empty cups, he positioned himself where he would be able to see Miranda exit the front door and walk to her car. He assumed she would leave early like the other faculty. But she remained in the house for a long time. He could not help glancing frequently away from Lucy to watch the door. "I'm going to California," he said, and, suffering through Lucy's congratulations and coos of possibly genuine happiness, he persuaded himself not to go inside and look for Miranda. Perhaps she had reapplied her makeup and had been delayed in the kitchen. One of the acolytes might have sought her out for an introduction to her parents. After half an hour, he glanced toward the house only to see Bernard approaching across the lawn with his aunt, both of them foolishly glad to see him.

"Here you are," said Bernard. "I was just telling Aunt Anne about Marquette and Joliet. Aunt Anne spent a summer in Marquette, Michigan, when she was a girl." Eventually, Roman became involved in conversation, and when he next looked up, Miranda's car was gone.

PART TWO

AN IMAGINED LIFE

—

ROMAN AND LUCY BOUGHT THEIR HOUSE FROM THE CITY of Lincoln. It had been repossessed from the previous owner of fifty years.

She was an aged woman who had never thrown out anything, hoarding thousands of objects for which she had no use. When Roman and Lucy first looked at the property, they were barely able to walk inside. The front room held hundreds of flower pots stacked wavily in fragile towers; three enormous crates of yarns ranging from pale pink to blackish purple; forty-five lamps; and a pile as tall as Roman of old *Omaha World-Herald*s. The woman's mania for preservation had left only a narrow path through the first floor. The second floor was entirely blocked.

Lucy insisted on this house. She had a vision of the place as it might someday be—its front porch restored and repainted, its floors refinished, its two sitting rooms pure and open, filled with light. It was a vision Roman could not see, but felt he must believe. "I promise you," she said, "that you won't have to do a thing." The bulk of the down payment would come from Ned and Sophie. He acquiesced, marveling that she required so little of him; and on the first of October, closing day, she hired a man with a truck who, in the course of one backbreaking week, simply moved everything away. She hired painters to scrape and paint the exterior; she hired two women to refinish the floor. When she was done, there was nothing else left of the house's former owner except for two of the best lamps and the faint impression of a footprint, small as a child's, sealed under the new varnish of the foyer.

Now the house was a gracious, almost empty space with high ceilings, wide maple floors, and an amazing stained-glass window that had been hidden away behind a stack of old trunks. Lucy cleaned the claw-foot tubs and brass door-knobs. She hunted down a few pieces of oak furniture that fit perfectly into the wide hallways and spacious rooms. Over the fireplace, they hung a red and violet sampler Emily had knitted with wool from the sheep of western Massachusetts. There were wedding gifts from Lucy's friends and relatives. The rest, Lucy said, they could fill up as time went by.

On their first night in the bedroom, Roman lay awake next to Lucy upon a new mattress, sniffing the pervasive, lemon-scented wood soap, listening to the occasional sounds of the house as it settled into winter. Occasionally there came, from the thoroughfare two blocks way, the shouts of drunken students straggling home. Roman turned restlessly onto his back. He took pride in the results of Lucy's work. Yet he was consumed by a thought that had occurred to him several times during the restoration, and now, on this first night, had myste-riously returned: it was a feeling, strong as a suspicion, that he had owned the house before. He had possessed this house, its tipping trellis and old flower beds; he had lived on this street with bare oak trees along the sidewalks and its woodsmoke smell of winter. Was this a homecoming? A repetition? Had he himself truly changed, with the winning of the prestigious Detweiler Prize, and then with his new job; or had merely the trappings of his life been changed?

He reached over and shook Lucy's arm.

"What is it, Roman?" she asked quietly.

"I don't know. I wanted you to be awake." He reached for something to say. "I suppose," he said, "that I'm impressing this upon my memory."

"Go to sleep, honey," she said, sliding a hand behind his ear. "You'll forget what you forget, whether you impress it upon your memory or not."

In the following years, he came up frequently against the rock of Lucy's common sense. She was by far steadier than he. When their son Avery turned three years old and Roman was consumed by a haunted anxiety, Lucy saved him by reminding him he had been three when his mother had disappeared. When Roman came up for tenure, growing snappish and enraged over the pettiness involved, she persuaded him that in his case the unpleasant process was a mere formality. She taught him that he was not as reasonable as he assumed himself to be. She sometimes teased him about this, and about how he had married her for her ability to ground what she called his flights of irrationality; but she did not know the truth he kept buried away from her: he had married her not for her clear judgment, her compassion, or even her beauty, but because he owed her a debt of gratitude. Gratitude for always having assumed the best of his poetry and of himself—for the surety of this belief that had granted him the possibility of a life in which he was not alone.

LUCY WAS A SPORADIC WRITER. Even at the School, she had suffered from self-doubt. She read too much criticism, Roman thought—which she seemed to use to find new ways of belittling her own work, although he never told her this. After Avery was born, whole months went by without her setting foot into her study, until gradually the room began to double as Avery's playroom. It was outfitted with a toy box and a brightly colored alphabet mat. When Avery grew older, Lucy's study was where he did his homework and put together his model planes.

Roman's private writing space was the attic. Sunlit and capacious, it was like a semi-finished third floor, easily accessed by a flight of stairs. The walls were painted eggshell white, setting off handsome old, dark slanting beams above, creating a kind of bird's nest to look up into during a moment of contemplation.

He wrote two collections in that attic: a second book of poems, published respectfully but with limited audience, and now, his third, *An Imagined Life*. This was a series of dramatic monologues from the point of view of his mother, Margaret—or, more specifically, of Margaret as he had come to dream of her, since he could not remember. This imagined Margaret spoke to the three men in her life: to him, Roman; to the unknown college classmate who had been his father; and to her own beloved father, Gilbert, a towering figure who had died of a heart attack when Roman was five years old.

Roman had grown up with a few signs of Gilbert's presence, such as the faint smudge over the doorway to the pantry—from which Roman recalled his grandfather had been tall and absentminded, like himself—and the smooth, hand-joined valet he had made himself—from which Roman had concluded that his grandfather, like himself, had cared for his appearance but was obliged toward thriftiness. Roman had little other knowledge of his grandfather, except what Emily had once said: "Your mother was always his. He had great dreams for her—it was his way of passing on his own frustrations. When she came home from college pregnant, he couldn't recover. Gilbert drove your mother away."

Decades beyond his death, the loss of Gilbert mysteriously returned to some vast interior memory that Emily could not share. She was plunged into a powerful, disjointed state. "Gilbert's been taken," she told Roman, over the phone. On other days, especially when the moon waxed or when the weather turned, she took to calling Roman late at night, wailing. Emily sleepwalked through the Monadnock Manor, her eyes as round and gray as stones, "visiting and upsetting," as the director put it, the other residents. Because of fire codes, they were not allowed to lock her into her room. The director called Roman to discuss the possibility of moving her. They did not have the resources to watch her any longer.

Roman fretted and worried. One morning, Lucy took

the phone away from him and spent half an hour comforting Emily. "She's lonely," she said, when she hung up. "Why don't we spend your sabbatical year in Massachusetts?"

She had wanted to have another child during this sabbatical. He was hardly able to express his thanks for her willingness to put the plan aside.

Roman spent the long winter seated beside Emily's wheelchair in the Manor's common room. He conversed with other residents while Emily took flight into the cloudy atmosphere of her own mind, gliding, drifting, occasionally reliving her marriage. Roman could scarcely listen as she grew lost in the stories Gilbert had told her about his service in the Pacific, plunging into a stream of phrases so aching, so disjointed, that Roman could not bear it.

"Purple heart. Purple heart. Purple heart."

Later, "They set the sword upon his neck, and raised it with both hands."

Roman understood that he had come too late. After years of missed holidays and brief visits, he had at last arrived for a long stay, but on most days she did not recognize him or Avery. She had given away her life in caretaking: of his uncle Skip, who had drifted to Portland, Maine, and was now of little assistance; of his mother, who had abandoned her; and of Roman, unfairly thrust upon her, whom she had raised with no complaint. He had not thanked her.

"I appreciate all of it," he said. "The meat loaf and string beans. Buying me so many tennis racquets." The longer he tried to talk to her, the more he understood that he was only trying for himself. "The sweaters you knitted, even with my long arms."

"Yarnover." Emily laughed.

"Did you ever hear from my mother again?"

"Ungrateful," she said.

Did she mean Roman, or his mother? There was a photograph album in a drawer; his mother as a girl, looking beyond him, even at that time, through lovely, strained dark eyes that seemed already far away. When he had last gone through the album as an adolescent, he had felt a naïve longing; but now, for a reason he could not discern, each snapshot was wrenching, each pose—Margaret at six, leaning slightly against the rangy Gilbert in his fedora; Margaret at fifteen, curiously exotic in the gray cardigan sweater and Peter Pan collar of her time, hands crossed in her lap, with the innocent, sure poise of a girl whose every gesture brought attention—each smile brought him to the verge of grief.

He understood now, viscerally, something he had only suspected as a child: that he was his family's aftermath. The most urgent betrayals, the great conflagration that had destroyed his family: all of it had taken place before he could remember, and the last traces were now burning out in the lightning synapses of Emily's winter dreams. Emily rarely mentioned Margaret, but on another afternoon, with gray sleet outside the window, she turned to Roman with eyes of stone and said, "You never saw the worst of us."

She died in August. In September the family returned to Lincoln so that Avery could start kindergarten. Roman recognized a truth: now that Emily was dead, he had no reason to ever live anywhere but Nebraska.

He asked Lucy if they could again postpone a second child, and she reluctantly agreed. He began to write—for a long, excruciating period without understanding, without form— then, finally, a few poems. Over the years, the poems began to make a sequence. He dug a trench into the process and stayed inside of it, waist-deep, sweating out the individual monologues, piecing them together. From inside the trench, there was no way to think of anything else: not marriage, not fatherhood. There was only the strength of voice, of words.

Sometimes he questioned himself. He wondered if this project was indeed the work of a poet, or instead was turning into that of a novelist: someone overly interested in the well-worn paths of narrative and time. He worried that he had lost his poetic imagination. But despite his doubts, the poems kept him going: he *knew* the voice now, and he felt certain that it was leading him toward something he wanted.

He sensed with an urgency, stronger than any kind of physical hunger, that these poems would make up a third book, and that this book held the key to the rest of his life. This was something he never spoke of to Lucy as they lay in bed listening to the crickets on long summer nights, never told Avery as he accompanied him to his baseball practice in the lot down the street, first as a five-year-old hitting from a T, then as a Little League player of increasing promise: that he desired a future for them beyond the Midwest. It was his responsibility to find them a way out. The opportunity, Roman knew, must lie in the book. It would be, it would have

to be, unusually good. As for what might happen if his vision
did not materialize, he refused to think. He tried to live as
frugally as he always had; and he kept upon his desk the slip
of paper from long ago: *All that matters is the work.*

When he had at last labored his way through the ordering
and revising, while checking the final manuscript before sub-
mitting it to his editor, Roman noticed something lacking.

It began with two lines in one poem:

You cannot know
The tie is irreplaceable

The lines explained too much, he thought. He changed the
lines to read:

You can know me
But the tie is irreplaceable

This was awkward. He changed the lines again and again.
The struggle lasted for days, until he understood that it was
not simply the lines that were wrong, but the entire poem.
Then another, related poem. Then another. Doubt spread like
an illness; one after another, the poems were found inadequate, until the heart of the project was infected.

Roman reminded himself he had the strength to over-
come this. Had he not pulled himself from nothing—with
no money, no support? Had his first book not won the prestigious Detweiler Prize? Hadn't he made a life, against all
odds, in an impractical profession? He worked each morning,

furiously, upon the poems, ignoring through force of will the insistent, growing fear—the fear that he could not, in actuality, write poetry. That he was spending his years like some blind, snuffling tunnel creature, pursuing nothing. In the long summer evenings, as the light slowly waned, he found himself in the grip of an anxiety he had never known. After a few more convulsive weeks, he felt, with certainty, that the poems were dead, their concerns both precious and false. He shut the manuscript into the lowest drawer of his desk and vowed not to look at it again.

IT WAS THE MIDDLE OF JULY, the exact center of summer, when he should have been making good use of his vacation time. But he had no tolerance for ordinary life. The raving cicadas bothered him; the humidity was unbearable. The garden's heirloom tomatoes lacked the flavor of years before. He cleaned his desk. He swept the attic; he alphabetized his books; he wrote and rewrote the syllabi for his fall courses.

He drove Avery three hours to Des Moines for a summer tournament. It was a point of pride with Roman that he rarely missed a game. But now, watching his son pitch, he realized that Avery had, unaccountably, changed under his eyes. The cornsilk hair curling from under his cap had thickened and deepened to dark blond. The bones in his wrists had grown prominent, and his hands, gripping the ball, were a man's hands. Still, the sight of him on the mound—pinned there, in plain sight—gave Roman something on which to focus. In the next two weeks, he drove Avery and his buddies to every practice, and took them out for meals afterward.

Then, on the first day of August, Avery, along with his two best friends, boarded the bus for a monthlong baseball camp in Woodland Springs.

His departure revived Roman's anxiety to an almost intolerable point. The house was silent and empty. Roman tried to read the newspaper, but he could not concentrate. He went upstairs, where he glimpsed Lucy sitting on their son's freshly made bed. It occurred to him that perhaps she might rediscover, in the weeks of Avery's absence, some pleasure in her own creative work. Now would be the time for her to find her muse. Roman turned away; he had not the energy to broach the subject.

He went to his attic, where he was reduced to drafting a new biography to appear next to his photo in the departmental handbook.

ROMAN MORRIS, *Professor of English and
Creative Writing*

Roman Morris is the author of *Night Words,* which won the 1989 Auguste Detweiler Prize for the most distinguished first book of poetry published in the United States. His second collection, *Auguring Steel,* was published in 1995 by St. George Press. He has been on the faculty since 1989. He is working on a new collection of poems.

Roman crossed out the final sentence. His claim of a new collection felt inflated, pathetically hopeful, and embarrassing.

He next crossed out the sentence about his tenure. No one cared how long he had been teaching. He had never considered himself much of a teacher. He had been offered the job in Lincoln on the strength of winning the Detweiler and he took it, relieved to be employed. He had, after all, no income without working. There had been no other clear path.

"Roman," Lucy said.

He looked up; she rarely disturbed him in the attic. But she did not seem troubled, and he looked back to his bio.

"I just got a letter from Bernard," she said. Roman heard a hum of lightness in her voice. "The legal tenant of his apartment died last week."

After a moment, he realized she expected a response. "That's too bad," he said. Yes, he would delete the sentence about the new poems. It was probable that nobody cared—and that anyone who did care had no occasion to read the bio.

"The apartment can legally pass to the tenant's daughter," Lucy said, "but the only way she can secure the rent control is to convince the authorities that she's been in residence for a while—I'm not sure how long—before subletting to Bernard again."

"That's rocky," Roman said.

"Until then, Bernard needs a place to live."

Perhaps he should leave the sentence in. It had, after all, been included in the bio for years, and its omission might generate unwanted attention. Perhaps he should simply leave the paragraph precisely as it was.

After a moment, Lucy's words registered. Roman looked up and saw her waiting in the doorway. Her face was vivid and her eyes almost green. "You don't mean here," he said.

She shrugged, girlishly, and with happiness. "For a month or two? It would be hard for him to make it out here, but we could send him the plane tickets for his birthday——"

"Where would he sleep?"

"Maybe we could bring up the foldout couch, and he could have this attic? That way we could all have a little privacy."

"What about my work?" he asked.

"Could you use your office at school?"

Bernard, with his pink cheeks and his unredeemable red tie; Bernard, who for a time had been the third voice in their conversations. Since graduation, he had been living in Manhattan, writing and barely making ends meet.

"It would only be for a while," Lucy added.

"All right," said Roman. "Call him."

"His phone is disconnected. I'll write."

Her footsteps tripped back down the stairs. Roman stood up and surveyed the room. He went to his bookshelves, looking over the thousands of volumes he had collected since he had begun earning a salary. He experimentally ran a finger along the binding of *Ideas of Order*. No dust.

Roman threw away his revision of the bio. Certainly he was at a point where he could not complain about giving up the use of his work space. In all honesty, the excuse not to write poetry filled him with relief.

He looked idly through his files. He could lock his papers before Bernard came, for the idea of privacy alone, as there was nothing worth hiding. The most intimate, expressive letters had come from Bernard himself. Since graduate school, Bernard and Roman had kept in touch by mail. Roman opened the folder of Bernard's correspondence. The letters were all handwritten in black ink on lined white paper; the first was dated September 3, 1987.

"I think often of that seminar," Bernard had written, in his precise, cramped script. "If you will believe it, I have been considering the comments made, by a number of the young women in the class, when we discussed an early draft of my poem. They said that one subject of the poem was homo-erotic love. I didn't think much of it at the time, because these contemporary phrases—so tinged by psychological cliché—mean very little to me. But over the summer, I have been remembering what they said, and it has occurred to me that the feeling of the two men in my poem is indeed a species of romantic love. In conjunction with this, I have been thinking about something Miranda once said. She said that the most memorable and significant relationships in literature have not typically fit into a conventional mode. She said that longing matters in literature, more than love. The power of that relationship which is undefinable. I have found something to this effect in my notes. Do you remember?"

Roman could not remember Miranda having said anything of the kind. But he believed Bernard, and Bernard's class notes. The idea troubled him. He had no desire to contemplate the significance of longing. Now that he was married, he turned to his marriage for love like most other people.

He must not have replied to the question; must not have

written back for months, for the next letter from Bernard was dated January 1988, and made another reference to his long poem.

"As a matter of fact, I am still working on the poem," Bernard had written. "At this point, I have taken apart the original draft I showed in class and I am working syllabically." He was counting out every syllable in every line, a process Roman considered needless and archaic. "I also spend a great deal of time on my correspondence project," Bernard's letter continued, "the project I told you about, that Thanksgiving. It's been absorbing me enormously, more than I expected. In addition, of course, I have taken a job at a coffeehouse to pay the rent. But there's no need for you to worry: I do think about my progress. I've always been a slow writer, and a bit exacting, and I must keep in mind that 'art is never finished, only abandoned.'"

A store-bought card came next, in an embossed white envelope. "Congratulations! Such good fortune! I'm overflowing with happiness that you two, who so deserve each other, have chosen to spend your lives together. It's so often the case, one hears, that a good friend becomes engaged to a person with whom one would rather not spend time. How lucky I am that my two best friends will marry each other. I offer my most affectionate wishes that you will find a world of joy in the perfect harmony of your union."

Roman rolled his eyes. He was proud of his marriage, but the phrase was so Bernard: "the perfect harmony of your union."

He must have filed the congratulations card hastily, for the next letter was out of order, dated before their engagement.

"I can't remember if I told you that I've done some traveling myself. I stopped in Bonneville as part of the trip to Aunt Anne's funeral. Since I so rarely leave New York, it seems wise to visit Bonneville whenever I can.

"I discovered, upon my return to Bonneville, how meticulously I have preserved that place in my memory. The particular value of the sky on a cloudy day in late winter; the shade and color of the light when the sun returns. The particular ratio of sky to earth, the way the small city lies in between. The *peep-peep* of icicles dripping, the squirrels venturing out onto the roof for sun. All of it moves me physically in the same way that I am moved when I encounter a photograph of my childhood. The power of memory is shattering. It feels so miraculous and strange to think that although I could go away and only sometimes think about this place, it could be preserved here—so self-absorbed am I!—as if for me. Being here again, finding these living memories, has helped me see that my time in Bonneville was crucial to shaping my heart and mind. I have known for quite some time that a very important thing happened to me there, and this visit only made this understanding more clear.

"I had coffee with Miranda, and it was wonderful. She was so beautiful, and more herself than ever. She also referred with fondness to our seminar, and she encouraged me to keep writing the long poem. We spoke at length about my new ideas for the poem and the way that Marquette and Joliet's relationship, so central to the story as I've described it, can never be preserved within recorded history. She spoke again about the significance of relationships that cannot be easily categorized by any official record. I was flabbergasted she even remembered the poem, and thrilled that she would think enough of the project to encourage it after all these years. I'm returning to my writing with renewed energy."

Roman slid the letters into their folder and locked them away. Let Bernard come upon the locked cabinet and assume it held his secrets. He wondered vaguely what important thing could Bernard be referring to. Perhaps he had once known, but he had forgotten.

Shaken by the details of Bonneville, Roman found a sudden need to defend himself against this coming visit. He knew that it was true that his marriage to Lucy had, in some inexplicable way, altered his correspondence with Bernard. He had found it far more difficult to share his thoughts, more challenging to disclose the details of his life, not knowing what Lucy had already told their friend. He felt a sense of privacy, almost injury, to know that she was closer to Bernard than he. Now it was often Lucy who contacted Bernard, Lucy who kept the two of them in touch, and he had no sense of what they spoke about.

Was it possible that, during the coming time of close proximity, Bernard might fall in love with Lucy? Roman's early confusion about Bernard's sexuality had somehow clarified over the years; and he felt sure that Bernard's significant attachments, if they existed, would be to women. Why not Lucy? Roman shook his head. If Bernard had been inclined, or able, to fall in love with anyone, he would have done it years ago. Not until after he and Avery had managed to angle the foldout couch into the attic did it occur to Roman that he had merely invented a way of wondering about the question that truly bothered him: whether it was possible to live harmoniously with a man who had been his good friend, but whose life's trajectory had, from his, quite drastically diverged.

BERNARD TURNED DOWN Lucy's offer of a plane ticket and took the bus. He would be making intermediary stops in the Midwest, he wrote, and a bus ride made more sense. He would be traveling for a week. For the length of that week, with Avery away at camp, no poetry, and nothing to do but help Lucy prepare the attic room, Roman imagined Bernard seated, reading, dozing, looking out the window. He remembered taking the bus across the country when he was young and unsettled: the stale air, the effort of redoubling his concentration on a book or notebook, the hundred tiny stops at a hundred rest stations. Waking up from a miserable night of awkward dozing as the bus slowed into a small hamburger stand in verdant, exotic fields of corn and soybeans. Stepping stiffly from the bus into the fragile, indeterminate atmosphere of a new place.

On the evening Bernard was to arrive, Roman left for the bus depot a few minutes early. He drove slowly with the window down, savoring, as if encountering it as a stranger, the delicate heat of a late summer afternoon, with the fierce and fragile light warming the lingering humidity. The faint sound of drums floated through the air. The university marching band had begun its practice for the year, and for the length of the autumn, depending upon the direction of the wind, the

blood of everyone in the vicinity of the stadium was stirred by
the steady rapping of snares. Reaching the depot, he searched
the stream of passengers that emerged: mostly students, tou-
sled from their hours on the bus, blinking as they waited for
their overstuffed duffel bags.

Amid the stream of students, Bernard appeared on the
top step.

It was with a jolt of emotion that Roman recognized his
friend: the slight, stooped frame, the faintly beaky profile,
which had only become more pronounced, more Bernard-
like, over the years. Bernard followed the other passengers
to the pavement and stood looking about him. His eyes were
bright, his cheeks flushed and still hairless, as Roman had
expected. He carried a worn brown valise, as Roman had also
expected, but instead of a tie he wore his shirt open at the
neck, revealing a small gold cross.

He examined Roman, minutely; then he smiled. It was the
same radiant smile, with its combination of delight and intelligent appraisal. "It's been years," he said. "It's marvelous to
see you, Roman."

But what did Bernard truly make of him, Roman wondered: years older, pounds heavier; and what did Bernard
make of this shabby bus depot, glazed in the pale gold light of
an early autumn afternoon?

For Roman himself was troubled by, unprepared for, the
changes in Bernard. Poverty in a young man is thoughtless,
presumably a visitor, and worn lightly. With age, it begins to
mark the face. Roman had not expected the lines about Bernard's nose and mouth, the features almost undernourished,

decidedly eccentric. Moreover, it was confusing to encounter, in the midst of these changes, the piercing, youthful quality of Bernard's gaze: that startling blue clarity, veering toward judgment, which Roman, feeling weary, now recognized as the extremity of innocence. Bernard, at forty-eight, was as good as a stranger, but at the mere sight of him Roman became aware of the compendium of his own life, organized by time as if in separate rooms of a house, precious items left to gather dust along with the clutter of years. A door had opened, old possessions uncovered, a part of himself.

At dinner, Bernard worked some magic in Lucy. Her eyes seemed very bright and her skin very smooth. She wore a dark green blouse Roman had never seen; around her throat shone an opal pendant set in gold that he had given her for her thirty-fifth birthday. The sight of her, both familiar and new, echoed some past moment of fulfillment and anticipation he could not quite recall.

That afternoon, she had roasted a chicken with rosemary and let the bird cool in its own juices; she had put together a great platter of fresh mozzarella with tomatoes and basil from their garden. A fragrant evening breeze poured in through the open windows, and long, late rays of sunset fell across the table, lighting the wine to gold. Words came unbidden into Roman's mind: 'There's a certain slant of light.' But why think of Emily Dickinson's late, despairing light of winter, when this light of a summer evening was so pleasurable? Roman felt wobbly with the pleasure of it all. As he sat mutely at his dinner table and studied the appreciative expression on the face of his guest, he understood he had attained the comfort he had always wanted.

"Where is your boy?" Bernard inquired. "Have you whisked him away so as not to frighten me? I'm not afraid of children."

"Child no longer," Lucy said, pride spilling into her voice. "He's not even thirteen and he's already like a teenager. He's at baseball camp near Kansas City—his first time away from home, for an entire week. You'll see more than enough of him, soon."

Roman worked the corkscrew into another bottle. It seemed dangerous to speak so blithely of Avery's absence: dangerous to let Avery drift out of their sight. He sensed that some mysterious cattail of fate might brush against their son and set him off course in a moment. Lucy did not understand. She missed Avery very much, but in the innocent way of a mother deprived of her child. To Lucy, Avery was merely away, joining forces with like-minded boys, though more perfect than all of them: straight and serious on the pitcher's mound, gilded in sunshine.

"And how is your work, Lucy?" Bernard asked. "How is the play you mentioned?"

A play? Roman studied the stitching on his napkin. Their unspoken policy had always been that Lucy didn't discuss her creative work with him; it was a policy he didn't try to change. He hadn't known she was writing a play.

As if she understood his discomfort, Lucy turned to him. "It's not much," she said. "I've been imagining a play about the lives of some poets."

"Which poets?" Roman asked.

"That's the thing about writing drama," said Bernard. "One has to come up with characters."

"Some poems also have characters," Lucy pointed out. She nodded at Roman and smiled, to apologize for having kept silent about the play.

"I suppose," Roman said, "that a lot of poets' lives contain plenty of material for drama."

"Tragedy, and comedy," said Bernard. He smiled and added, "Just make certain you avoid rhyming it."

Roman, hazy with wine, enjoyed the echo of the drinking game at Oscar's. He leaned across the table and kissed Lucy on the cheek.

"You should write your play," he said. "You have the time now, with Avery growing up."

Lucy said, following a moment of silence, "After all, it's only an idea."

"A good idea," Bernard insisted. He raised his glass. "To the success of your play," he declared, tipping his glass against Lucy's, and then Roman's. They drank.

"To all of our success," corrected Lucy. Roman saw the hectic flush on Bernard's face—when was the last time the poor guy had had a sip of wine without a wafer?—and he felt a welcome glint of answering happiness.

THEY PILED THE DISHES in the sink and strolled toward campus, so that Bernard could get his bearings. They reached the long main street. It was still quite warm, and Roman could smell the undergraduates milling around them: sweat and cheap perfume, new, warm yeasty beer, and stale beer.

One of Roman's students approached: Veronica. Roman cringed. She was a small, wan, troubled girl, whose surprising gifts as a writer seemed to have been granted along with a commensurate burden of anger and self-doubt. She came to office hours frequently and, despite Roman's firmest resolutions, often engaged him in virulent speculative conversations, interjected with observations about the class that felt like criticisms. She had made the past spring semester challenging; and, to his dismay and, oddly, to his satisfaction, she had registered again for his fall class.

Now, upon the sight of him, she nodded sullenly. "Hi, Professor Morris," she said. Roman nodded back, feeling awkward.

Bernard weaved a step ahead along the sidewalk.

"I am quite drunk," he said. "And a thousand years old. If I weren't here with you, I would be lost."

"Don't worry," Lucy said. "As you can see, it's quite normal to wander about this part of town in an inebriated condition."

"I do see it," Bernard said. He turned to Roman. "You included me in the toast, but aside from my tenuous hold on a sublease to a rent-controlled apartment in Manhattan, I don't think I have achieved, or even will ever achieve, the kind of success that you're thinking of. Although I do feel rich in friendship." His eyes were shining with feeling. Bernard went on, "If they never abolish rent control in New York City, my current degree of success is assured for life. But I'm in trouble if they do."

Was he warning them that he might someday need a place to live? "You could housesit," Roman said. "Or take a job in insurance, like Wallace Stevens."

"Although I have great admiration for Wallace Stevens, I can't imagine looking for, or working at, that kind of job."

"No doorman, then, for you," said Lucy. "No master bedroom, no fancy countertops, no six-burner range. You write poetry, remember?"

Roman listened to her talk, faintly envious. He wanted the master bedroom, the doorman; he wanted the city. But this was not to be his life. While he held his tenured job in Nebraska, the great, burnished island of Manhattan would hum its symphony of financial and artistic work without him.

Bernard smiled. "That's right, I'd forgotten, we write poetry. Roman, Lucy, why *do* we write poetry?"

Roman said nothing.

"You never know what the future will hold," Lucy said.

"Believe me," said Bernard. "In my case, I do know."

Lucy laughed. Roman allowed himself to remember that night so many years ago, at their classmates' holiday party. He had stood with Lucy near the bar, and she had laughed with similar delight at Bernard's bow to Miranda. A sweet, girlish sound, a sound of earlier times, a time of newness he'd forgotten, or that he did not know he'd had.

He reached for Lucy's hand and squeezed it. Her hand was warm, comforting.

As if he could somehow detect the nature of Roman's thoughts, Bernard asked, "Have you spoken to Miranda recently?"

Roman kept a mindful hold on Lucy's hand. She wore only her wedding ring. "Not for years," he said.

"You don't stay in touch?"

What was that in Bernard's expression? Was it merely curiosity? Or something else, something very un-Bernard, similar to envy? For a moment, Roman wondered if Bernard knew all about the nature of the relationship he'd once had with Miranda. This could not be true, since they had been so careful; and Bernard had lived such a circumscribed life in Bonneville that there was no way he could have discovered it. Moreover, Bernard was incapable of suspecting such a thing. Perhaps his friend's expression was merely disapproval. Perhaps Roman had broken some unspoken code of decent conduct, as if Miranda were some aged relative to whom Roman had failed to send an Easter card.

Roman let go of Lucy's hand and pushed his fists into his pockets. "You keeping track?"

Bernard blushed. He was clearly uncomfortable, but he persisted. "It's just that when we were in school the two of you seemed—I thought, certainly you were close—"

Roman kept his voice light. "You're wrong," he said. "Occasionally, I used to let her buy me dinner," he said, and forced his lips into a smirk. "Jealous?"

"Not at all!" cried Bernard.

Roman was suddenly aware of Lucy, and he winked at her. "What about you, Bernardo?" he asked. "I remember the way you danced with her at the holiday party, our second year. Are *you* 'in touch' with Miranda?"

"Well, as a matter of fact," said Bernard, "I am. We write

regularly, and on the way out here, I stopped in Bonneville, as you know. She and I met twice, for breakfast and coffee."

Stung, Roman said, "Do you write to her as part of your correspondence project with the great poets of our age?"

He was not prepared for the silence that followed. When he finally looked at Bernard, he saw an expression of consternation. Surely Lucy must know about Bernard's correspondence project, but Roman suddenly wondered, with a pang of guilt, if he was betraying some confidence he was not aware of having entered into.

"I ask if you've been in touch because—I thought you might have heard," said Bernard. "Miranda and her husband were recently divorced. He has remarried, to a much younger woman, another architect, I think. When I visited, she seemed somewhat isolated. I think she'd appreciate hearing from her old students."

They were walking past a campus building. A group of students played Frisbee on the lawn, thoughtlessly moving in the dusk. Roman watched as one boy, fleeter than the others, followed beneath the floating white Frisbee like a shadow.

"I should write to her," said Lucy.

"That would please her, I think."

No more was said. Relieved, Roman turned the group back toward the house. He'd had enough of Bernard: enough for an evening.

But when Roman took Bernard and his suitcase upstairs to the attic, his guest had no interest in saying good night. He held out his arms to the room in astonishment at their generosity; he looked at the ceiling and the slanted eaves, at the desk in the window, then at the pulled-out sofa bed, made up with one of Lucy's quilts.

"I'm afraid I'm putting you out of your work space, Roman. My deepest apologies."

Roman shrugged. "You'll put this space to better use."

Bernard moved to the wall that held Roman's books. "Are you writing much these days?" he asked, scanning the collection in a way that vaguely irritated Roman.

"I'm almost finished with—something," Roman said.

He could not explain how it was the case that for all the years he'd struggled, he was not making any progress. He stood staring at his desk. It looked like a stranger's desk, certainly not a place where he'd sat for hours each morning, for all those years. The pile of poems in the drawer, written by a stranger. "What about you?" he asked.

"Still writing my long poem. It's wonderful that you have new work."

"Sure," said Roman, automatically. "It's in the bottom drawer of the desk, if you're interested."

"Thank you, I look forward to it. Also, may I borrow this book? Just for something to read while I'm here. I've left my copy at home—"

Bernard was holding Roman's copy of *Flight*, the gift from Miranda.

Roman hesitated. He had not opened the book since one afternoon shortly after graduation, in a fit of sentimentality upon receiving the class portrait, which he had long ago misplaced. He didn't want to lend the book, but it seemed odd not to. And he knew that once he did, Bernard would leave him alone.

He took the book from Bernard, examining it. On the back cover was a black-and-white photograph of Miranda at thirty-one. He knew her age because he had once used the benchmarks of her career as checking points for his own. He had seen the photograph many times, but now, in Bernard's company, he could not look at it for long. She seemed luminous with life, in the way she had when dancing or, sometimes, making love; and Roman felt a sudden heaviness in his head and lungs.

"Go ahead," he said. He thrust the book back into Bernard's hand.

"Roman," Lucy called from below, "did you bring the extra quilt up there?"

"I have it, thank you," said Bernard. "Good night."

Roman, hearing something in Bernard's voice, glanced at his face. It was drawn, private, infinitely sad. Roman said good night and walked—tiptoed, almost—downstairs.

So Bernard would put himself to sleep that evening not with Proust, but with Miranda's early poems about the gift of loneliness. Roman considered this as he lay next to Lucy, waiting for the heavy feeling to recede. Since his first night of insomnia in that house there had been others. He told Lucy he worried about his poems, which, while not entirely the case, helped explain his behavior. Now he got out of bed and made his way to the kitchen. He often roamed the house at night, prowling through the closets. To explain this, he told Lucy he was looking to see if there were any hidden cupboards or cabinets the movers had missed, any spaces in that house concealing a thousand grocery lists, or seed catalogues, or blenders.

Roman halted in the kitchen, transfixed by the glowing square of moonlight on the tile floor. It was a struggle to believe that he was almost forty-five years old—much older than the woman on the book jacket. She must now be more than sixty. This was impossible, and it seemed impossible that she could be left by Michael, by anyone. He had not heard from her in more than a dozen years, not since that terrible conversation after he had won the Detweiler. Their estrangement had been complete.

IN THOSE DAYS, the Detweiler was quite possibly the only award given to a young poet that might be known to the general reader. After writing in such solitude and anonymity, Roman was surprised by the attention. Lincoln and Syracuse wrote inviting him to apply for jobs. There was a profile, with a photograph, in the *San Francisco Chronicle*. There was an interview in *Poetry*. There was even a small piece on National Public Radio, with a brief live interview that ran the morning the prize was presented. The awards ceremony brought Roman to Manhattan in late September, where he stayed with Bernard for a week.

It was a year of great change. Upon his arrival in New

York, they went uptown to meet Lucy for dinner. True to her agreement with Bernard, she'd moved to the city shortly after graduation.

Roman almost staggered when he saw Lucy rise to greet him in a polka-dotted dress, joyfully calling out his name. He found her altogether bewitching. The sight of her long-lashed hazel eyes and her pretty, smiling mouth—and the affection in her voice and in the touch of her hand—evoked a poignant feeling, almost nostalgic, akin to longing. He felt suddenly that she had been saved for him, a trusted friend and a woman yet unknown: a companion from the past who possessed, quite possibly, the potential to come with him, forward, into the future. He had not known how lonely he had been.

When he sat down, she studied him wonderingly from across the table. "You look older," she said. "Almost more thoughtful, grown-up. Or perhaps that's only because you've gotten famous." Roman sensed it would not be difficult to arrange a private meeting. There followed a furtive phone call, a plan for lunch, and, with some guilt, a decision not to invite Bernard.

On the morning of his date with Lucy, Roman sat in Bernard's one chair, browsing through the latest issue of *Poets & Writers* while brimming with anticipation and with the struggle of keeping a secret. Bernard sat working in bed, eight feet away. It was the only other place to sit in the apartment. True to Roman's expectations, his friend's room in Manhattan was even smaller than the one he'd had in Bonneville. Its cramped size made all conversations ongoing.

Bernard was scratching away at a letter to a poet named

Joshua Turpin, who lived alone in the Memphis bungalow where he had been born. Bernard had discovered Turpin in a small letterpress magazine from the South. Turpin wrote only in certain old forms—a strategy considered rigid and obsolete—and, to make his verses even more obscure, he wrote very slowly. He was particularly fond of the pantoum, and his pantoums were haunting, exquisitely turned. Each was a minor masterpiece. It was a shame, Roman thought, that nobody but Bernard seemed to appreciate them.

Bernard drafted his letter in a spiral-bound notebook. Every few minutes, he would set his pen down carefully and stare out the window at the brick wall a few yards opposite.

"How about this?" he asked, and began to read. "'I was quite sorry to learn about the death of Jeoffrey. I can only imagine how significant he was to you—how enriching and fortifying his company has been over the years. He was, from every description you have given me, a cat whose magnificence and unique personality will be missed—missed by all who knew him, but especially by you, who have been his loving caretaker and his particular, cherished human friend.'

"You know," Bernard continued, turning to Roman, "I've often imagined that it must be a terrible experience to lose a pet. Others might not have seen the value in the pet—might not appreciate that its loss might be as devastating, if not more so, than the loss of many human companions. There exist such communions that are irreplaceable." Roman thought he had stopped talking, but after a moment, he asked, "Do you think I've made that clear?"

"Absolutely," Roman said.

He turned back to *Poets & Writers*. He'd been informed, by someone at the awards ceremony, that the Detweiler people had taken out an ad for him.

Searching for the announcement of his prize, he stumbled across an interview with Miranda. She discussed her new book and how her work had changed when her mother took ill in the last year of its composition. She also revealed that she had been the chair of the jury for that year's Detweiler. Roman read the sentence once, then again.

It was as if she had given him the prize, then taken it away.

"Bernard," he said.

Bernard looked up from his letter. "Is something wrong?"

Roman hesitated. It felt inappropriate to bring up the subject with another former student, but with whom else would he discuss it? "Nothing, really," he said. "In this interview, Miranda said she was the Detweiler jury chair this year."

Bernard's pink and white brow wrinkled with concern. "You didn't know?"

Roman, who had been surprised to see *Poets & Writers* in Bernard's room, realized that his impoverished friend must have purchased it only because it contained the interview with Miranda. And so, very likely, would others among her former students. Everyone from the School would know that he had won the prize because Miranda had chosen him.

"No," he said, "I didn't know." He tried to shrug, although he found it difficult to breathe. "It's no big deal," he said.

Bernard went back to his book. Roman glanced through the rest of the issue, but the articles held no significance.

Even the announcement of his prize, including his name and the title of his book, meant nothing.

Hours later, in Lucy's studio apartment, he told her about the interview. He wanted her to hear about it from him, exactly in the way he wished.

They were lying in her bed under an ecru comforter, watching the city traffic far below. The faint sound of traffic drifted up into the room. The move to her place, and then to bed, had happened immediately after lunch, where neither of them had eaten much.

"I just found out," he said casually, "that Miranda judged the Detweiler this year. That was odd." To show her this was not significant to him, he laughed. But his laughter fell into the room with some awkwardness.

"You didn't know she was the jury chair?" Lucy asked.

Roman shook his head.

She scanned him carefully and he noticed, in a new way, how pretty she was, especially the fresh color of her full mouth and the way her long eyelashes tangled at the corners.

"I wouldn't worry," Lucy said. "No one who reads the poems will think that favoritism is involved."

Roman remembered the way she had defended him in graduate school. Tears came to his eyes, shocking him to speak.

"Thanks," he said. He was filled with emotion and confusion. The confusion had to do with so much happening at once. The prize, the possibility of employment. This new-found connection with Lucy, kindling a sense of happiness and relief, a sense of hope, that he had never felt with anyone.

The gut-socking recognition that he owed all of his good fortune to Miranda.

"What is it, Roman?" Lucy asked.

Roman hesitated. He wanted, with an urgency that seized his bones, to tell Lucy everything that had happened. He must tell Lucy because she was his friend; and because she would understand, more than Bernard, how complex and troubling it was. Yet he could not speak. The information, with its implications for their fragile shared world, would change everything between them.

Roman shook his head. "It's no big deal," he said, and pulled Lucy to him more closely. Then, because he needed terribly to change the subject, he began to make love to her.

AS HIS PUBLICATION date drew near, Roman grew frightened of returning to Bonneville, as if he would be entering the kingdom of an enemy.

He wrote Miranda that he would be in town to give a reading, staying at a hotel. "I'm sorry to hear about your mother. I learned the news in New York, where I also was informed that you were the chair of the jury for the contest," he wrote. "Thank you for your help. Winning the prize means"—and here, he paused, before finishing the sentence—"a lot to my career."

He soon received a response. The note was written on a fine, cream-colored card embossed with Miranda's intertwined initials in dark blue ink. "I was delighted to support your wonderful work, Roman," her letter read. "So happy

you are coming to town. May I take you out to a congratu-
latory dinner?" Roman, shaken by the sight of her familiar
handwriting, did not reply.

Certainly he was one of only a few. Not everyone came
back, and most not with a book in hand, to give a reading.
After checking in at the hotel, Roman walked toward the
School along a street paved with the fallen petals of crab apple
blossoms, and as he breathed the air fragrant with the crushed
petals, he thought about Bernard's ecstatic letter. "The particular ratio of sky to earth, the way this small city lies in
between." He remembered the smell of the air in the final
spring when he had lived in Bonneville. He had gone around
town every day thrumming with the secret of his entangle-
ment with Miranda and the secret that would free him from
it, taking in with every breath the scent of loss and possibility. Now, as he walked in her direction, he found it difficult to
keep putting one foot in front of the other.

He was careful to visit during Miranda's office hours. As
he approached, he saw her door was partially open. She sat
reading; she was frowning at a student manuscript (he had
learned, during their affair, that she did actually read them),
her desk positioned so that she could see into the hallway. He
thought it ironic that when she had been his teacher, he had
not come to her office hours, had rarely seen her like this.
Her office was like any literary stranger's, filled with books;
an asparagus fern he had not seen hung in the window. She
looked severe in her wire-rimmed glasses, her hair pulled into
a knot, but at the sight of him, she broke into a radiant smile.
To his surprise he felt an answering, pure happiness.

"Roman, I'm so thrilled to see you. I've been wondering forever how you were."

Bernard had written that Miranda was more beautiful than ever. Roman saw that she had aged noticeably—especially about the eyes and mouth. Even so, the joy and pleasure in her gaze, and the effortless, bracing quality in the way she moved toward him, drew him. She shone like a candle; and like any light in the darkness, she made him believe, for a long, forgetful instant, that he would be safe within her radiance. He felt he had been traveling alone in the world, and had found shelter. Such keen intelligence, such understanding, such willingness to look out for him in ways small and large, such belief that he would be all right—it was still there inside Miranda, there for him. How could he have forgotten?

She came around the desk to hug him for a moment, then released him and stepped back. The blood came into his feet and hands. They had held each other so many times, and his body could remember it.

Miranda sat lightly on the edge of her desk, tipping her head back to look at him. Yes, he was fine. Tired? A little—and it was strange to be in Bonneville again. He could feel her sincere, almost sweet fondness with each question.

"I made reservations for dinner at Waterstone's," she said, "but we can change them if you'd rather go to another restaurant."

"Dinner?"

"Did you get my card? I thought we could have an elaborate, celebratory dinner."

"We've never had dinner out before."

"You're not a student anymore. Of course, if you'd rather——" She stopped, and looked up at him, perplexed.

Was there a strain of forced gaiety, of expectation, in her voice? Suddenly he felt exhausted. He wished with all his heart that his return to her could hold the innocent happiness of Bernard's. But it could not.

And it angered him, in a way he could not explain, that she could assume that dinner out between the two of them would be seen as innocent. Had it been a thousand years ago, or had it been only yesterday? What they had done was irrevocable, and yet her statement implied that there were rules for managing the aftermath of such things, that she had navigated these waters in the past. It was likely he was not the first student with whom she'd been involved. This suspicion had hardly come to him when he realized that it had been there all along, and that he had pushed it away.

He had no desire to learn these rules. He must stay out; he understood now that he had barely escaped.

"So we're all clean now?" he said.

She was examining him——his face, his hands, his clothing—— happily, in the minute, particular way he now remembered, with the look of a lover and a caretaker, but when he spoke, she heard his ironic tone and drew back slightly.

He tried not to flinch at the sight of her injury. He said, trying to keep his voice light, "Isn't Waterstone's a horrible name for a place where people supposedly go to eat delicious food?"

She was watching him more gravely now. He found something familiar in her troubled gaze——the feeling that he must disappoint her and that she would never understand precisely why he must—and at this recognition of the feeling, a feeling he had had half a dozen times, with half a dozen women, but never more acutely than at this moment—he felt a wave of sadness crush his chest, as if she had cast a spell to drown him without water, and he could not breathe. He struggled for what seemed like ages, shocked by its force. He could scarcely stay there in the doorway; he must cut this short.

"Let's talk now," he said. "These are your office hours?"

"All right," she said.

He left the door open. There were only two chairs in the office, and he sat on his side of the desk, hoping she would make her way to her own, official, side. To his relief, she did. This gave him the advantage of a certain formality. Miranda offered him a cup of tea, and he refused. She asked if he wanted coffee, which he also refused, and pushed a box of Russian chocolates—gifts from a student—at him from across the desk. Roman did not touch the chocolates.

"How was your flight?" she asked, after a long silence.

"It was fine."

"You must let me take you back to the airport tomorrow. I'll meet you at the hotel. When—tomorrow at six a.m.? They have only that god-awfully early flight out on Saturday morning."

"Sure," he said. It would save him twenty dollars.

What could they talk about? They had never conversed in pleasantries. There were no small subjects: only poetry and time. He had taken pride in this, considered it honesty. Now he understood the value of small talk with its comforting banalities.

"I saw Bernard Sauvet," he said, "and Lucy Parry. Bernard came to the awards ceremony."

Miranda nodded. "How are they?" she asked. It seemed to Roman that she could not quite place which classmates he meant.

"Fine." He wished that he could tell her about the relationship that had grown between himself and Lucy—the meeting in New York, the hours spent in her apartment, the ensuing phone calls and visits: the relief, the surprise and yet inevitability of their feelings, and the sense that this was the right thing for him. He wanted her approval.

"I didn't know you were the principal judge of the Detweiler this year," he said. "I found out about it in New York."

Miranda waited, long enough for a deep breath. "When I received the finalists' manuscripts, I wanted to let you know I would be supporting yours," she said. "Bernard sent me your address, but I didn't write because I was told I could not contact you until after the prize had been approved by the board. At that point, you already knew."

"You never struck me as someone who was interested in following the rules," he said.

"What do you mean?"

He took a deep breath; it was time. "Surely there must be a rule against awarding the prize to former lovers," he said.

"Roman—"

"Is there?"

"Are you questioning my decision?"

"I suppose I am. Why did you give me the prize?"

"I wanted to be supportive of your work."

"Why——" He looked away from her, toward the bookshelf. He was having trouble keeping his voice even. "Why did you want to be supportive of my work?"

"Why, because you were a brilliant young poet on the verge of publishing an important first book," she said, as if, in his doubt, he had affronted her.

Roman shook off her words. He found that he did not know whether to believe her. This discovery rattled him more than anything. "So there wasn't just the tiniest feeling that——"

She waited, staring him down.

"——that you knew that if you gave me the prize, we would have to be in touch again?"

"Roman," she said, "I didn't even come to the awards ceremony."

He recalled hearing that her mother had died. Her mother was dead. That accounted for the weariness about her eyes and mouth. She had lost her mother. He could not think about it now.

"But you didn't know, at the time you made the decision, that you would not be able to come."

Miranda was shaking her head. "I didn't know that this would upset you so much."

"The point is"——he was breathing hard, trying to form the thoughts that he must share with her, words that he must say, had been waiting to say for months——"the point is that my poems *deserved* to win."

Miranda looked at him, puzzled. "They did," she said, as if it were obvious.

Roman went forward with his line of thought. "They deserved to win," he said, "and now people might think that they did not."

"Who are these people?"

"People. People who knew you were my teacher and people who suspected us of—of something."

"I've never said a word to anyone."

"I haven't either, but now this choice makes everyone think we were—involved."

"How do you know that?" she asked, exasperated, but Roman could not stop. He understood, now, what had been upsetting him about this trip, and although he wished to flee the room, he knew that he must tell Miranda. She alone held the key to his understanding of what had happened.

"Why did you tell *Poets & Writers* that you were the chair of the jury?"

Miranda said nothing. She looked baffled, and, Roman suspected, worried. He waited long enough for several heartbeats, until he could not bear the silence anymore, and he continued.

"It was supposed to be confidential," he said. "I know, no one said it had to be confidential after it was announced. But you decided to tell."

Still, she said nothing. She was watching him with an apprehension he had never seen on her face before. Roman went on.

"The thing I have been wondering is: *Why* did you tell? Because when you did, you must have known that everyone would read it. You knew that I would read it. Did you want me to find out? Did you want me to be grateful? Did you want me to express how grateful I was to you?"

When the words were out of his mouth, he had the sickening feeling that they were true. Miranda could not undo her hair to hide her face, and so she looked away, revealing the long line of her neck. She sat in that pained position for some time. Roman thought, Surely someone will walk by in the hall. Someone will see her looking like this, and they will know. He leaned over and shut the door. At the sound of it closing, he felt that he was hiding from the entire School something shameful and wrong.

"And how did you want me to express my gratitude?" he asked.

In the silence that followed his question, he felt himself breaking away from the conversation, rising up, out of the room, circling far above the two of them. It was a feeling of deadly certainty, something akin to triumph.

"Roman," she said finally, "how can I explain it to you so that you'll understand? When you're my age, you'll understand. But you don't know that yet. How could you know that? You're young and handsome and so talented—your entire future is still ahead of you. That spring—that graduation. When you left town—you left with scarcely a goodbye—" She paused, and said what he had waited to hear. "I missed you so much."

"And so you gave me the prize."

"That's not true! It only seems that way to you—"

"But there isn't a tiny bit of truth to it?"

She did not answer. Suddenly he needed, with a need bordering on desperation, to know the answer to his question. He understood he might have gone too far, to a point where even he did not wish to take the conversation, but it was too late.

"Tell me if there's any truth to it," he said, and he hated his voice; it was as if he were pleading.

She drew a long breath. Roman hoped that she would lie. But she had never lied to him. Not about poetry, not about what mattered. "Yes," she said. "A tiny bit of truth to it. But only the smallest bit, and only partly true."

Now that she had said it, now that he had forced her to say it, he found he could not respond. He could not think of a word. He saw the desk blurring before him. He put his head into his hands and felt, to his great shame, wetness on his fingertips.

He understood that her greatest appeal to him had been the faith he had put into her opinion of what was good and what was not. Yet he had felt, also, a tearing need to know that she had missed him. How these two basic sources of feeling had become so treacherously entwined was incomprehensible. How would he live with this? How could he outlive it?

And how could she look so wretched, so vulnerable and sad? He saw that she had suffered, in these last two years, without him. For a moment, he suspected that if he could simply make it through one long evening with its slow meal and conversation and perhaps its lovemaking, then he might survive this shame. He might reach the other side of it, go to the place that beckoned, had beckoned—some place of understanding. But perhaps it might not. Such an experience—even the consumption of the smallest meal together—might lead to a deep and pointless exposure of some dreadful knowledge. And it would tie him, inevitably, even more tightly, to Miranda. This, more than anything, might plunge him into a bottomless emptiness he had worked so hard, had employed all of his strength, to avoid.

Miranda stood. "Roman, please, I'm sorry—I should not have said that."

"Maybe there are a lot of things you should never have said to me."

"Roman, I made a mistake."

Why had she not protected him from knowing this?

"Roman," she said. "The book is a great success. What's more, you're doing wonderfully: every poetry journal, even the mainstream presses think the book is extraordinary."

Her words meant nothing to him. He could no longer believe them. "What mattered was always what you would think."

She came around to his side of the desk. He flinched. He did not want her to touch him.

"You'll learn from this," she said. He heard in her voice a desperate unhappiness. An unhappiness that, to his dismay, he desired with all his heart to ease. But he must not help her. Any sustenance he offered her would diminish his own strength; if he took one step to comfort her, he would be lost.

He swallowed and controlled his voice.

"I suppose," he said, "that this is also part of my poetic education."

She closed her eyes. He yearned to see her the way she had appeared when he had known her only as a teacher: to return to those moments in class when she had looked at them all through her indifferent gaze, when it was impossible to know what Miranda Sturgis had been thinking.

"But it's true," she was saying, and now her eyes were also filled with tears. "You will learn from this."

"In what way do I learn from this?"

"Please believe me. The people who matter the most to us in the end, who teach us the most, are the people who make their worst mistakes with us."

"And why should I believe you?"

"Please. You always believed me."

He began to tap on her desk, a comforting, rhythmic insistence of his presence. "Of course, I suppose you'll say in class that what matters is still beauty and truth. I used to sit in class and wonder at the way you refused to take note of what was happening around you. But even artists are responsible to others. Especially teachers."

"I'm not perfect," she said.

"No," he said. "You're not. I suppose you knew that if you gave the prize to me, maybe I would come back through town to give a reading. We could have dinner and screw around."

She made a small, involuntary sound.

He could not stop tapping on the desk.

"It won't work, after all," he said. "Sorry. I'm booked up tonight." He shrugged. "Bernard didn't tell you? It turns out I'm seeing someone."

For a moment he waited, almost hoping for an appropriate reply, such as "That's great news," or "I'm happy for you." He wanted her to give her blessing in the same way she had congratulated him when he had told her he was going to California. But she did not speak. There was no argument between them anymore. Frightened, he tried to start it up again. He said more things—angrier, truer things, but Miranda did not respond. She simply sat looking aged and diminished. Roman steeled himself to feel no sympathy. Wordlessly, she moved her hands, still graceful, always graceful, reaching for her pocketbook. She was looking for her car keys. She was going to leave. No, perhaps she planned to stay; perhaps she was only looking for her crimson makeup bag, with its little round compact mirror. He had seen her use it a hundred times. She was still searching her pocketbook. Roman could not bear it one more second.

He pushed back his chair. "Don't feel bad," he said. "I'm sure there are plenty of other handsome, *very* talented young men in your classes. I'm sure they will be ultimately more teachable."

"You meant the world to me," she said, unsteadily, but purposefully, as if this were a statement she wished to put on the record.

He stood.

"Goodbye," she said, looking up at him, absurdly old.

IN THE FOLLOWING MONTH, as he gave readings from college town to college town, he thought over and over of writing to her, but each effort led to a struggle of shame and unhappiness. Finally he gave up thinking of it. He would let things cool down. He thought that when he finished his reading trip, he might contact her, but he did not. Nor did she contact him, although, he reminded himself, with some sense of injury, that this impasse would undoubtedly come to an end. Surely, they would someday run into one another at a writing conference. They would be cordial and accept one another in the manner of old lovers. Moreover, Roman felt on some level that nothing *had* changed. Deep down, nothing that had been said would change it—the puzzling and undefinable thing—the essential attachment between them so incomprehensible and so unspoken that he rarely cared to think of it.

Had it not been the crux of their attachment that he was the pupil and she the instructor? She had been *meant* to introduce him to the world and to his future.

BERNARD HAD BEEN in Lincoln for a week when Roman drove alone to pick Avery up at camp, fighting that shyness he had often felt toward his son since Avery had begun to grow, so rapidly and almost unaccountably, the year before.

Playful wrestling and teasing had its place, but Avery's approaching manhood—and Roman could see it in the wariness of his eyes, the sudden vulnerability in his step as he grew taller—had created a need for conversation. He had never known anyone more minutely than he knew his son. It seemed to him that he had witnessed Avery's every desire, and every caution, since he had come into the world. Always he had given encouragement and advice. But now, as he helped Avery load his enormous equipment bags into the back of the station wagon, as Avery entered on the passenger side and folded his new, long legs into the car with surprising care and agility, Roman said nothing. He could not talk to Avery, could not disclose the contents of his own mind to this suddenly thoughtful young man, the son for whom he was responsible.

He had bought Avery a gift: a baseball glove that had cost three hundred dollars. He had chosen the glove with care, consulting a colleague he disliked who had been a minor league player of some promise before he entered the academy. He had endured the superficial ribbing and backslapping of a conversation with Hal Committo in order to find the glove. The glove was in the backseat, in a plain shopping bag.

"How was camp?" he asked.

"Good."

"Fun?"

"The coach was great. He made us think."

Roman pushed forward. "About what?" he asked.

Avery paused, and then continued. "I did a lot of thinking about my future."

Awkwardly, he pushed again. "And—what have you been thinking?"

"I'm considering the career of a major league baseball player."

Roman kept his hands relaxed on the wheel. A tenth of a mile passed, then two. What to say? To mindlessly agree? Or to point out that only a fraction of all aspirants reached this goal?

"That's good," he said finally. He looked across the passenger seat at his son. Avery was watching the freeway with a hungry awareness. Roman knew that he looked forward to seeing his mother. Roman could not help asking, "And what is your Plan B?"

"What do you mean?"

"Everyone needs a Plan B."

Avery turned a puzzled glance upon him. It was the wondering, lovely gaze of an innocent young animal, and Roman decided not to pursue the issue.

He would not wish for his own complexities to be shared with anyone. He wanted Avery to remain innocent, free of his own ambition; but if Avery *must* have ambitions, he wished that his son could escape his own turbulence. Roman switched on the radio and tuned it to the Royals game. As he and Avery made their way home, listening to the game, he wondered if his inability to share his thoughts was caused by the ill-adapted wrongness of his own head and heart, or whether it was simply in the nature of being a father. He did not know; he had not known his father.

They reached the house, and Avery left the car, trying to conceal his excitement at the prospect of seeing Lucy. Roman reached into the backseat and removed the shopping bag. He would find another moment to present the glove.

Bernard and Lucy were in the kitchen making pie crust. Lucy's apron was spotless, but Bernard's was splotched with flour, and he had smudged flour on his nose and on his glasses. Roman felt awkward as he made introductions, wondering what the future ballplayer would make of the eccentric visitor who would stay for an indeterminate amount of time. But as it turned out, he had no reason to be worried.

"You're a friend of Mom and Dad's from graduate school?" Avery exclaimed. "I didn't know that they had any friends."

Bernard was charmed.

During dinner, Avery sat next to Bernard and examined him frankly. He had inherited Lucy's openness, as well as Lucy's winsome hazel eyes. "You wear a cross," he said. "My coach wears a cross. He says he wears it in order to stay out of trouble. Are you out of trouble?"

Bernard smiled at Avery, delighted by the question.

"Bernard is not in trouble frequently enough," said Roman, but no one laughed.

"As a matter of fact," said Bernard, "I do get into trouble, much more often than your father would believe. But my trouble won't get me punished by my employer or rejected by my neighbors. It's internal trouble, really. And so I wear the cross to remind myself who I want to be. For various reasons, related, really, to my own unworthiness, I don't go to Mass anymore; and so I need to remember. Sometimes I become distracted, and need very much to be reminded."

Avery said, "I know exactly what you mean!"

"Do you?" Bernard beamed.

"When Coach mentioned it, I got the feeling he's afraid something bad will happen *to* him. From the outside, like a truck is going to hit him. Your trouble comes from the inside."

Roman said, "Would anyone like more bread?"

Lucy smiled at Roman. She set her foot against his, under the table.

"Yes—it's more like trouble with myself," explained Bernard, addressing the table generally.

Roman stood up and went to get the bread. He would eat it himself.

Afterward, in their bedroom, he said to Lucy, "Is Bernard giving Avery lessons in theology?"

"Bernard said that Avery is beautiful," said Lucy. "Like a candle, he said."

"He wants to pitch in the major leagues."

"A worthy goal."

They undressed, got into bed. Lucy placed her hand lightly on Roman's thigh and they lay together, silent for a moment. Roman thought of Avery in the next room and Bernard in the attic. As was typical on Saturday nights, he could hear drunken students on the main street two blocks away.

Lucy said, keeping her voice low, "I just realized when he mentioned it at dinner that so far on this visit, Bernard hasn't been to Mass at all. I wonder what happened. Do you know?"

"No," said Roman. He also wondered what internal unworthiness had sundered Bernard from the Church. He had seemed open enough in mentioning the subject to Avery, but Roman thought it might be awkward to ask.

"I don't want to pry," Lucy said. "I thought that he might talk to you—that maybe man to man, he wouldn't insist on so much privacy."

"I thought he'd be that way with *you*," Roman said.

"It's an unwritten rule of our friendship. We talk about

everything to do with daily life, and with poetry and poets, but we never bring up religion or romance."

He wondered, but only briefly, why it was that aside from discussions of his work, he and Lucy did not talk about poetry and poets. He asked, "Did you talk to Bernard about how long he's planning to stay?"

After a moment, she replied, "Not yet. Have you?"

They now heard two young men shouting from a distance, one merely loud and the other in a voice hoarse and uncontrolled, in the throes of some great, youthful unhappiness.

"Well," Roman said, trying to keep his voice reasonable, "I figure this issue is something you've dealt with before. Bernard living in your place, that is. Back when you moved to Manhattan, didn't he crash with you until he found his apartment?"

"We never discussed when he would leave."

"How long did he live with you?"

"Two months."

"And you never discussed it?"

"I knew that when he no longer needed to stay, he would go."

"I suppose he was a damper on your sex life."

Lucy made a slight sound that might have been another smile in the dark. "As a matter of fact," she said, "I was glad that he was there. If he hadn't been on the couch, so filled with solicitude and conversation and moral fiber, I might have gone back to Max again."

"I didn't know you and Max were still an item after grad school."

"Not officially." Her words seemed to echo. Roman's foot itched, but he ignored it, so as not to interrupt her. "With both of us in New York—"

Her sentence was broken up by the noise of the drunken students outside. They had turned off of the thoroughfare, and were, for some reason, heading down this quiet residential street. The miserable, hoarse cry of the one young man clarified itself. "So, I'm a slut!" he yelled. "I'm a whore! I'm a slut! I'm a slut!"

"Good grief," said Lucy.

"It doesn't seem like the kind of situation you would let yourself get into," Roman said. "You and Max, that is."

"He—attracted people. He had a way about him." Lucy paused. "My primary attachments seem to be with very attractive men," she said, and touched his shoulder in the dark.

Roman could hear an apology in her voice. He understood that she considered the news of her prolonged relationship with Max to be a source of possible pain for him. But he felt only curiosity and a kind of compassion, almost relief. "He broke up with you," he prompted.

"Yes."

"You kept seeing each other, after that."

"For more than a year."

No wonder she had been so keen to leave New York, when they were married. Roman thought about her vision for their house, clean and filled with light, the old clutter gone.

"I wanted to be married," Lucy said. "I wanted children. But he always said he didn't want a family, ever."

Roman tried to remember if he had heard anything about

Max's progress as a poet in the last dozen years. "Does he have a family now?"

"No. He's kept his vow to live a life for the sake of art."

"How do you know that?"

"Bernard told me. They see each other now and then, at readings in the city."

Roman had no reply to this. He did not know whether to be jealous of Max, who lived this life for the sake of art, or pleased with himself for giving Lucy something Max would not. He turned over and made ready to sleep. But as he began to relax, the young man's hoarse cry echoed from farther down the street.

Lucy shifted. "Roman, since we're on the subject, can we talk? There's something I've been meaning to bring up."

Although she spoke evenly, Roman could sense the focus that lay beneath her calmness.

"What is it?" he asked.

"Well, Bernard told me that you'd finished your manuscript. If you remember, when Emily died, you and I discussed—"

"I'm not quite finished with it yet," he said.

"Bernard thinks it's finished."

He was annoyed that the two of them had been discussing him, his work. "He read it?"

"He did," Lucy said. "He thinks it's finished."

"Then why hasn't he told me?"

"The reason I bring it up," Lucy continued, with uncharacteristic impatience, "is that we'd talked about having another child, when the manuscript was finished. I'm almost thirty-eight. We may not have much more time."

Roman remembered the conversation now, years ago, also at night, in bed. He said, "I was upset. My grandmother had just died."

"Are you saying you didn't mean it?"

"That's not what I'm saying." He searched quickly for some way to move from the discussion, but Lucy's tone was grave. He thought of her putting her foot against his, under the dinner table. Clearly their thoughts could hardly have been in more different places. "It's just that I don't know if I want another child," he said. He had never said this before. But now that he had spoken, he knew it was true. The postponement of years had only clarified his misgivings on the subject.

There was no sound from Lucy.

"I mean that I haven't thought about it—haven't thought that we would have another child," he said. "Avery is just growing up—and don't you want more time?"

"What do you mean?" He could hear, behind the question, some quickening in her mind, an alertness making her voice quite still.

"More time to write, I mean. You get so absorbed in being a mother." He heard her draw a breath. Now he had put his foot in it. He tried again. "I mean that I would have thought you would welcome this time ahead, time for projects—like your play," he added hopefully. "Time without distraction, time to think about your work, only your work."

"You mean that that's what you want," she said, and he knew there was no point denying it.

"Can we talk about this later?" he asked.

Lucy did not reply. Roman reached for her but she, almost predictably and yet still shockingly, moved to the far side of the bed. He lay where he was, wishing he could take back what he had said. Yet he knew that Lucy would have guessed the truth.

IN THE FOLLOWING WEEKS, Lucy remained cool to him, and Roman did not try to approach her. It *was* difficult to have a talk with Bernard in the house. Difficult to consider the complex and gray-shaded concerns of marriage, parenthood, with Bernard's somewhat otherworldly presence at each meal. Bernard set a great store by ideal behavior, Roman knew; and there was nothing ideal about being the inadequate and awkward father of a boy reaching adolescence, a middle-aged man who had come to a perplexing bend in the path of his marriage. Nothing ideal about a job teaching creative writing to a mixture of hungover, and troubled, and occasionally gifted undergraduates. Until Bernard moved in with them, Roman had not recognized how much of his time he spent at teaching, or thinking about its often petty concerns.

Though Bernard didn't teach, he contemplated the annoyances of Roman's job with a detached generosity.

"Of course you should read it," he said, when Roman complained one evening over dinner that, although he was not her advisor, his student Veronica had asked him once again to help her with her senior thesis. She had deposited herself at Roman's door, in tears, asking for his help. It seemed she could sense that he had no work of his own to do that fall.

"I'm sick of it," Roman said.

Bernard looked at him, vaguely troubled by his tone.

Roman tried to redeem himself. "I mean that I've read it so many times I don't think I could see it objectively, even if I tried," he said.

"Oh. Well then, by all means, you should tell her you won't read it again."

Lucy said, "She only wants attention, Roman. She probably has a crush on you." She wagged a finger at Roman in a way that made him wonder if she was mocking him. "You be careful," she said. "I know the type. Looking for help from the cute teacher."

Roman shook his head. He had been pursued by under-graduates before, but Veronica was different. He felt not quite pursued, but used; and yet he was also seduced, not as much by Veronica herself as by the work. Lucy had not suspected the true appeal of Veronica, the oddly beguiling way she had with her turns of phrase, her lucid and disturbing observations.

"It's not that simple," Roman said. "She's troubled. Her novel is a thinly disguised memoir about her struggle as a teenager with anorexia."

"I think it's very kind of you," said Bernard, "to give your students so much personal attention; and impressive that you know so much about their lives."

Bernard had no idea of how times had changed. He had

seen their teachers as monolithic, mysterious forces of nature rather than as people. To such a force of nature, one made sacrifices; one prayed; one served as an acolyte, faithfully and for years, until one was given some sign that one had moved to a higher level. Miranda—here, Roman remembered the way she had been when he had first sat in her classroom—had been talked about incessantly precisely because she revealed so little of herself, and it was assumed that her teaching style, with its long silences, its pronouncements, and its drastic judgments, was justified by the fact that she was, indeed, Miranda Sturgis. If some of her students prospered and flourished, it was almost as if they had managed to flourish *despite* Miranda. (The shy, plump Shannon Bruno, in fact, had become a published poet, fairly well-known in a theoretical coterie, and the recipient of a good academic job in Southern California.) No one expected to be noticed by Miranda; certainly, no one expected to be taken by the hand and *mentored*. If he and Miranda were still in touch, he might have asked if this had been a deliberate tactic: if she had believed in this indifferent behavior as a method of making her students put more effort into their poems.

Nowadays, Roman thought, the students expected not only to be noticed, but that their work—however absent the vision, however awkward the execution—be discussed with the assumption that the goals were far-reaching and accomplishment inevitable. Moreover they felt that they were owed these services, as their professors' end of an official transaction. Many believed that writing could be "taught" by the dissemination of "craft," and that anyone with the smallest speck of ability or desire was entitled to this dissemination. No one bludgeoned anybody anymore. One could write with utter mediocrity, but one had the same right to be treated as if greatness, or, at the very least, publication, were imminent. In Roman's first years of teaching, he had struggled against what he perceived of as this silent insistence on mediocrity, putting aside his own time to write with a sometimes brutal authority. But now, he was not writing; he had nothing else to do but to teach the mediocre.

Veronica was *not* a mediocre talent. Her gift for language was considerable and her eye for detail unusually acute. Her struggle with self-starvation had given her a lot to write about. Her renderings of her physical battles were wrenching, agonistic; but she lacked the ability to string those glittering, raw moments together into coherent lines.

Roman spent half a dozen exhausting conferences extracting transitional sentences and paragraphs from her disorganized manuscript. He had rarely found himself doing this kind of prose work. He tried to find a prose writer to help her, but one fiction writer was on leave that year and the other, as a consequence, was overworked. Veronica's advisor, Roman's colleague and friend Spencer Davis, was the other faculty poet. Roman possessed a penchant for narrative; while Spencer, a much more lyrical and impressionistic writer, was unable to offer the same kind of help.

Each two-hour bout with Veronica and her manuscript left Roman wrung out and astonished at the audacity of this young woman, who came to him for help as if she were working on a problem set and wouldn't leave until she had written down each answer. But as he labored over her novel, he began to feel a certain pleasure in seeing it come together, in the knowledge that he had played an important role in its completion. What Roman did not tell Bernard was that he felt an unfamiliar, perhaps new, *responsibility* to Veronica—not to her personally, exactly, but to her manuscript. He had begun to find a pleasure in teaching, despite what it had cost him in blood effort.

One afternoon in late October, as they struggled over the final chapter, Veronica began to sob in his office for perhaps the seventh time.

Roman sat on his side of the desk watching her shake miserably, her face in her hands. Her fingernails were bitten down, the cuticles ragged, but despite this absence of care, her trembling hands were curiously beautiful. It occurred to him, and not for the first time, that if she had been his student in another era, all this working together might have led to intimacy. He might have had an affair with her, and this moment would have had a different tone entirely.

Instead, he handed her a tissue.

It was now believed, by everyone in the academy, that a sexual or even a romantic relationship between a teacher and student was an abuse of power. There were rules now; a man in Roman's own department had lost his job over a kiss. His colleagues had been outraged. Some had felt the man was a monster; others that he was being forced to pay too much for a moment of weakness. Roman had said nothing. He did not know if the rules were most helpful in preventing a student from suffering abuse or in avoiding a situation where

the other students watched jealously from the outside, knowing they were learning relatively little, while one of them had
access to so much.

IN MID-NOVEMBER, Roman met with Veronica for the last
time. She would graduate in December, and he would never
again have an obligation to her or her writing.

Veronica arrived at their meeting in a tight pink sweater,
revealing collarbones painfully suggestive of her adolescent
malady. Because of her wispiness, she appeared younger than
her age. There was something pieced-together in her expression, as if she had already given away a part of herself in a
bargain that, at the time, had mattered very much, but was
now long forgotten.

Roman expected her to talk about how glad she was to
have finished the thesis, but instead she folded her hands carefully in her lap. Roman tried to think of something to say.

"Well, Veronica," he said, "you'll be graduating in two
weeks. Are you excited? Worried?"

"I'll be glad to leave school," she said. "The academic aesthetic is more narrow than mine." She eyed Roman in a way
that had grown familiar to him, half indifferent, half challenging. "I think it will be good for me to have other influences,"
she added.

Roman wasn't entirely sure how to respond to this.

"I have good news, Professor Morris," she said, primly.
"Do you remember I wrote to an editor at Simon and Schus-
ter last spring?"

Roman nodded. She had queried the editor, who had requested a first chapter, and she had spent the ensuing summer revising in agony, unable to show him anything. Roman had tried to describe to Bernard this paradox of her smug ambition and terrible insecurity. Bernard had found the anecdote baffling, insignificant.

"Well, I sent him the revised chapter two weeks ago. And he sent me this letter."

She held out a business envelope. Roman noticed again her trembling hands, the nails bitten down. After a moment of confusion, he understood that she wished him to read the letter. He reached out and took the envelope.

It was a longish letter from a well-known editor in New York, praising Veronica for her beautifully written, wrenching story and for her unflinching honesty, and asking to see the rest of the thesis.

"This is wonderful," Roman said. "Congratulations."

"Yeah, thanks."

He reached awkwardly for what advice a novelist might give. "You might want to look for an agent."

"I think I will. I would appreciate the kind of feedback an agent could give," she said.

"Still, I hope you've found my feedback helpful," he said.

She did not reply. She gave him an appraising look that he remembered from class, a frank examination from a young woman that inevitably made him feel very old. Then she shrugged, and reached into her pocket for a tissue. She blew her nose. A tag of light hair escaped childishly from her headband.

He felt obliged to say something more. "You should be proud," he said. "And this may remove some of the typical postgraduate confusion for you."

"Actually, I'm glad I'm graduating," she said, sniffing. "I found this to be a somewhat stifling environment for a writer. I think it's time for me to be in the world."

Roman swallowed, struggling to think of the appropriate thing to say. "Well, it was a pleasure to work on your project."

"Thanks," she said. It was a moment before he realized she was thanking him not for his help with her project, but for the compliment to her work.

Without another word, she stood to leave. When the door had closed behind her, Roman sat for some time without thinking, trying to recover from the violence that had just been done to him.

At dinner, Bernard said, "Of course, she's extremely grateful for all of the help you've given her."

Roman said, "She'll be an excellent novelist: a monster of self-absorption."

He berated himself for caring. Why should he mind that the publishing industry would burn through another young talent? Of course, he had to admit that his jealousy had to do with the fact that he was not writing; he had no desire to write. He had put all of his energy, it seemed, into *An Imagined Life*, and in the following week, he began to think perhaps the book was really done. Bernard still hadn't mentioned a word to Roman about having read it. If Lucy had not told Roman, he would not have guessed that Bernard had even opened his desk drawer. But despite his own disappointment with the poems, Bernard seemed to think the book was done.

That Saturday, after Bernard and Lucy set off for the final farmers' market of the season, Roman climbed up to the attic and retrieved his manuscript from his desk drawer. He put it into his briefcase, took it to the post office, and mailed it to his publisher.

THANKSGIVING PASSED, marked by even more lavish preparations than usual on Lucy's part. There was an organic turkey ordered from the food co-operative. There was a soup concocted from local produce: leeks, red peppers, and heirloom potatoes. There was cornbread, made days in advance for the experimental cornbread stuffing, and there was "regular" stuffing for Avery, who, despite his relative newness to the holiday, viewed any deviation from tradition with skepticism. Then a fleet of additional side dishes, finished off by pecan pie, which was Lucy's own idea of a Southern dessert.

Roman ate and drank enough to fill himself; and then, conscious of the need to perform to standards of Thanksgivings past, he ate and drank as much again.

While serving the pie, he and Bernard told Lucy and Avery the details of the Thanksgiving they had spent together while in graduate school. The cheap wine, the burnt, oozing grilled cheeses, the chilly apple turnovers.

"It was abysmal," Bernard concluded.

"It sounds like fun," said Avery, slightly puzzled. He had eaten every spoonful of the regular stuffing. Now he drooped with uncharacteristic drowsiness, his cheeks flushed and his hands spread on the table in front of him.

"But you see, this is far better than grilled cheese," said Bernard, beaming at Lucy, his own face poppy red with warmth and wine and food.

"Then I've succeeded," said Lucy.

Roman thought that perhaps Lucy had wished to shower upon Bernard the cornucopia of plenty in order to make up for every previous year he'd been deprived. With such a need to nurture, such generosity, it was no wonder she wished to be a mother again. Sitting at the table, his head swimming after the egregiously large meal, he began to believe that all things might be possible. It might be possible that he would someday write another poem. It might be possible that Avery, with his innocence, his determination and discipline, would develop in his heron-like arms and legs the strength and skill required for major league baseball. It might be possible, might even be pleasant, to go through the years-long household upheaval of a new child again. Certainly, he had little else to work on at the moment.

But in Thanksgiving's aftermath, Lucy did not bring up the issue. Perhaps she had had second thoughts. Roman felt guilty for the way he had first reacted. He tried to make it up to her. He gave her time alone with Bernard, when they presumably discussed subjects such as Lucy's old relationship with Max Zabor. He encouraged Bernard to tell Avery over dinner about the nature of goodness. As the weather grew chilly, he drove Avery to his indoor conditioning sessions, questioning him, and listening carefully, about his ambition to be a ballplayer. Without being asked, he cleaned the house, sequestered Avery's droppings of sneakers and equipment into orderly rows, tidied his own detritus in the bedroom closet. He waited expectantly.

On a Saturday morning in early December, while straightening the room that doubled as Lucy's and Avery's studies, he came upon a manuscript on Lucy's desk. For a queer, suspended moment, he thought it might be a work of her own—the product of some effort she had not revealed to him—but one glance proved otherwise. He sat down at the desk and began to read.

He had not finished the first few lines of the poem before he found himself drawn in by its voice. He sat down and read urgently, forgetting about his plan to rake the last few oak leaves from the yard, and his promise to Lucy to collect the recycling. He was barely aware of the emotion growing as he read: his breaths coming shallower, his mind ringing with wonder.

Roman finished the whole manuscript, and then reread. After some time, he surfaced to the sound of the front door opening, then voices. It was Lucy and Bernard, returning from the library. He did not want to see them; he could not yet control his confusion. He took the back stairs down to the recycling bin and hastily loaded the car.

It was not until late afternoon that he had chance to speak to Lucy alone. By then he'd had time to think, and he chose his words carefully. "I have to apologize," he said. "I was cleaning up and found Bernard's manuscript. I couldn't help reading it."

She glanced at him sideways, unimpressed by the reference to his cleaning. "Oh? What did you think of it?"

"It's wonderful," he said, and his words felt inadequate. He was consumed with jealousy and at the same time an almost metabolic joy: the joy of having discovered something rare, something worth reading. Truly, he felt as if the top of his head were taken off. "It's more than wonderful," he added. "It's astonishing."

"Miranda told him that if he really wanted to make it perfect, wanted to make it as good as it could be, and for it to become the great work of his life, that he should give it a few more years."

"Miranda said that?"

"Isn't Miranda allowed to give advice to Bernard, as well as you?"

Chagrined, he said, "I don't know what you mean. I was surprised, I think; that's all." He was more than surprised. He was troubled; he hadn't yet been able to sort out the reason. Bernard's long poem was too beautiful; the shock of reading it still recent. His mind rang with the certainty that he had just discovered, from an entirely unexpected source, a work so plaintive and so lucid, so particularly of its own devising, that he would not recover from its reading for some time. It was a work created from a deep, unusual inner world, a world for which much of ordinary life must have been sacrificed. This, rather than impressing Roman, annoyed him; how had Bernard known? How had he had the confidence— the arrogance!—to sacrifice so much?

"Are you going to tell Bernard?" asked Lucy.

"Tell him what?"

"What you think about his poem."

Roman considered this. "I don't know."

"Don't know?"

Was her voice a little cold? Roman winced; he had the sense of digging deeper into trouble. "It's simply that—you told me, a while ago, that he read my book," he said gingerly. Once the words were out, he felt petty and fatuous.

"Yes?"

"I suppose I assumed that if I showed him mine, he'd show me his." It sounded silly when he said it. "And yet," he said, struggling to understand the reason for his anxiety, "Bernard and I spent a lot of time talking, and he never talked about showing me his manuscript. I wonder if it had something to do with how he felt about my manuscript. You said he read it, but he never spoke to me about it."

Lucy's glance was brief, but challenging. "Why don't you talk to him?"

ROMAN THOUGHT for a week, a long week. He taught his final classes, held his grading conferences, and suffered through the composition of several letters of recommendation for Veronica, who wished to attend writers' colonies and apply for fellowships. Each evening, there was dinner and conversation with Bernard, whom he could not help seeing in a new way. Now the oddities of Bernard, which he had once thought charming, rankled. Why, for example, did Bernard not learn to drive? Did he feel himself to be above such mundanities? Was he saving the strength, wasted by others on transportation, for his poetry? He thought about Bernard sleeping for two months in his attic, reading his books, sitting at his desk. Suddenly it became intolerable that he would have no use of his desk during the remainder of Bernard's visit. Each morning, he found himself pacing in circles in the bedroom, directly below the desk, imagining Bernard seated there, making his usual minute notes in pencil.

On Friday, Roman suggested to Bernard that they drive to Omaha for lunch. "I don't have class today," he said, "and you've hardly seen the sights, although you've been here for almost three months." The words were hardly from his mouth when he realized that three months was a *very* long time, and Bernard's visit of punishing length.

The temperature was dropping rapidly, too soon for the season, and the gray air felt heavy with an impending shock of early winter cold. They parked in a garage and walked to an Italian restaurant Roman knew, where he and Lucy had gone on a few special occasions. He felt obliged to choose a good restaurant, obliged to make the meal expensive. Since he had finished reading the long poem, his friend had taken on a kind of weight and stature in his mind. He ordered a large meal and persuaded Bernard to help him with a bottle of wine. As they ate and drank, they discussed the books some of their classmates had recently published; they talked about Roman's colleague, Spencer Davis, as well as some poets Bernard had met in Manhattan. Bernard said nothing about his long poem, or whether he had heard news of his apartment, or when he was planning to go back to New York. When they were finished, Roman picked up the check.

As they stood to leave, he said to Bernard, "Lucy tells me you read my manuscript."

Bernard turned slightly away, troubled. "I didn't mean to keep it from you—" he began. Then he pulled his gloves from his pocket. Roman wondered if they had discussed more about the manuscript than Lucy had revealed. The heaviness of the lunch, the strength of the coffee, made him wish he had not introduced the subject.

"I know," he said. To forestall Bernard's opinion, he thinned and lightened his voice, to imitate the question Miranda had asked long ago. "'Is this a poem?'"

Bernard looked at Roman, then at his gloved hands. "It's poetry," he said.

Roman waited, and when Bernard did not elaborate, he felt himself on the verge of trying to express the suspicion that had been growing in him over the summer. He had told no one of the feeling, not even Lucy, and he had the sense only just now, and with this listener, of being able to put it into words. "It's not poetry," he said. "It's gnawing on the bones of poetry."

Bernard said, winding a narrow red scarf around his neck, "Its insight and breadth is extremely impressive, and the voice is much more convincingly rendered than in any work I've seen of yours before."

"But you don't like it," Roman asserted.

"I didn't say anything like that."

"But you don't."

They left the warmth of the restaurant reluctantly and set off down the street, toward the parking garage. While they were at lunch, the weather had turned suddenly to deep winter, and an icy wind drove into them, bringing water to the eyes.

Bernard bent his head into the wind. His expression, Roman thought, was strangely aggrieved, or perhaps it was the cold. "It's not quite that, Roman." His voice seemed to echo more loudly outside of the restaurant. "Your poems have become in many ways, astonishing, really."

"But you don't think I've improved much, do you, over the years?" Roman's own voice rang, with an uncomfortable clarity, against the iron-cold sidewalk.

"I—I—well, I have an odd opinion about all of this, as you know."

"What do you mean?"

"To be honest," Bernard said, "I don't think that most of us ever truly improve."

They entered the imposing ramp where Roman had parked the car. As they climbed the stairs, Roman felt a dull pulsing behind his temples. He stopped walking for a moment and waited for it to recede. There was something almost menacing in Bernard's words that made it difficult for him to think. "What do you mean by that?"

Bernard spoke slowly and evenly. "I don't think we get better, during our lives. Most of us get worse. And the others—well, perhaps they write better books. But they don't 'improve.' Our truest limitations are not technical. I said it years ago: poetry cannot be taught. All of this instruction of technique is merely superstition, magical thinking—wishful people tinkering over a decision made for them long ago."

"That's not true," Roman said, cutting off the thought with a gesture of his hand. But he himself had often wondered about this question. "Of course it's possible to improve from learning craft," Roman continued, lamely.

"It's possible to write a better book, perhaps, but not to become a better poet."

"Give me an example."

"From our generation? Well, Bob Lu. His last collection had some lovely poems, but you can't say he has improved, or even lived up to the promise of his early work."

Roman drew himself up to argue. It was *not* true; not in every case. For one thing, *Bernard* had become a better poet. His long poem was stunning; in the years since graduate school, it had transformed from something slightly pedestrian, or even dull, to a shining, beautiful object, a shimmering design of words and images. But Roman could not say this to Bernard. Bernard had very deliberately kept the poem away from him.

Moreover, it seemed not through an accrual of craft that he had grown. It was not craft, but a sense of surety, as if during those years, in his isolation, Bernard had refined from his anachronistic forms, his distant friendships, and his suffering—for Roman suspected now, there had been suffering—a piercing clarity of feeling. This was poetic vision. No amount of craft could ever make up for it.

"Where is the car?" Bernard asked, and Roman was suddenly aware that he had no memory of where he had parked.

He thrust his hands into his pockets. The cold was penetrating, raw even in the garage, where the wind raced between levels. The concrete numbed his feet. For several minutes, he walked silently up and down the rows of cars. Bernard followed uncomplainingly, although his corduroy coat was, Roman noted, too thin and too short for winter in Nebraska. But *would* he stay for the whole winter? Roman, stopped short by the question, forgot for a moment if he had taken his car or Lucy's. And had he, Roman, not improved as a poet? How could he ask Bernard about this?

"But you think it's true," he said, his words making shameful puffs of steam. "You do think it's gnawing on the bones. You do." They had reached the end of the second floor. "Damn," he added, "I was sure I'd parked on the second level."

They climbed, colder every moment, to the third level. Roman felt, again, the blood throbbing in his temples. He took a deep breath, trying to calm himself, but his stubborn, unspoken question lingered. After a moment, Bernard said, "You could show it to Miranda. I'm sure she'd love to see it. It would be a comfort to her to read such fine work from a former student. And she would tell you what you need to know."

The name, coming unexpected, assaulted him. "No," he said.

"Are you angry at Miranda?" Bernard asked.

In his own way, Bernard had fumbled toward the problem. He was not precisely correct, but he was too close.

"It's complicated," Roman said. He clenched his hands in his pockets; he could not feel his fingers, but his head was pounding now. "My work was never her favorite, if you'll remember from class. I've moved beyond her, aesthetically and in a number of other ways."

"I don't mean to intrude," Bernard said, "but I have sensed for some time that you are upset with Miranda, and from something you said long ago, in New York, I have suspected that your concern has to do with an impression of yours that she at one point in your career attempted to be possessive of your accomplishments in some way."

"I never said that," Roman said.

"You didn't in so many words. But it has seemed to me, as I have learned more about the lives of many artists and their most important teachers, that there can come a rift in the relationship at the point of emerging, where the student begins to feel that the teacher assumes too much credit, if you can call it that, for the achievements of the student. I know that she was proud to have worked with you but I'm sure that she in no way expects to be thought responsible for your success."

Roman gritted his teeth. "Look," he said, "we just had a kind of falling-out."

"How did that happen?"

"Long ago," said Roman. The cold had seized him up, and he was shaking. "When we were only a few years out of graduate school."

"You haven't contacted her since?"

"I don't see any reason to do so."

Bernard's teeth chattered, but he spoke clearly and decisively. "Well, this might be a good time to do it. You might want to let her know that you appreciate all of the help she gave you. She *was* largely responsible for getting you started out, you know."

It was one of the few things Bernard could have said to hurt him. Moreover, Bernard must *know* that it would hurt him; why had he said it?

Roman said, "And you think I owe her a debt of gratitude? And that she would be happy to hear from me, despite our falling-out, after all these years, as long as I make it clear to her that I approach from a position of gratitude?"

"Yes."

"And I suppose you know all about that, Bernard, from your years of experience in human relationships?"

Bernard looked up at him, pinched and shivering, hurt and not bothering to hide this hurt. It was this lack of guardedness, this almost aggressive lack of it, that bothered Roman most of all.

He turned away. There, in the far corner, was his car. It needed a wash, although, Roman assumed, Bernard would not notice or care.

They got into the car, shaking as they sat down upon the cold, cold seats. Roman turned up the heat, producing a loud and irritating blowing sound. They began to wind their way slowly out of the garage.

Bernard sat in the corner with his red nose in his scarf. He had brought a palpable sense of injury with him. Unable to control himself, Roman pushed further. "Why won't you tell me what you think of my new poems?"

"Roman, I don't understand why you are so determined to hear my thoughts."

Roman paused, perplexed by a sudden, inexplicable fury. He felt truly sorry for the lunch, sorry he had embarked upon the conversation. The garage was crowded with winter shoppers. They drove in circles, with several cars waiting at each turn. The air was thick with exhaust. It was torture, Roman thought. It was taking forever.

"Because I want to know what you really think," he said, finally. "It's more than that: I *need* to know."

Bernard shook his head. "Why do you *need* to know?" he asked. "What could you possibly need from me?"

"Come on, you owe it to me," Roman burst out. "You've been living in my studio for three months."

Bernard straightened in his seat. His eyes were very blue and his cheeks still red with cold.

"I'm sorry," he said.

"I didn't mean that," Roman said. "Come on, Bernardo. You know we're happy to have you here."

"I do owe you," Bernard said.

He was staring straight ahead, eyes fixed past the windshield. Roman felt suddenly afraid of what he was about to say. He clenched his hands around the wheel to keep from shaking.

Bernard drew a deep breath.

"I think this next manuscript will be well received."

Then Bernard paused, seeming to think exactly how to put

his thoughts into words. "If you wish me to be absolutely hon-est, Roman, I suppose my thoughts don't have to do with *An Imagined Life*, specifically. I've simply wondered, generally, about your choice of the form of the dramatic monologue."

Roman opened his mouth, but before he could formulate his question, Bernard went on.

"You're good at it, extraordinarily good, so good that it should not have to matter. But I wonder if there might be something—well, territorial, or even boastful about the form itself; I mean in the idea that one could inhabit the subject matter. As if, by speaking as others, one might become so cer-tain, so in control, that the imagined world—when the book is read—is a bubble that glistens, untouched by life." Here Bernard paused again. "Although the mother is permitted to speak, she speaks not as herself, but as the poet wishes her to speak. The things she says are things the poet wishes her to say. Roman, your *self* is never present in the poems. You seem to risk nothing."

Now Bernard was reaching for his pocket. Roman won-dered if he was looking for a handkerchief. His own head was ringing, as if he had been struck.

They had arrived at the booth. Roman fumbled to roll down the window, then handed the ticket to the attendant.

"That'll be two dollars and twenty-five cents," the atten-dant said. With their meandering in the cold, the car had been three hours parked in the garage.

Bernard thrust some bills at Roman.

"I'm paying," Roman said. His voice rang loud and flat in the small space.

"I have the money," Bernard said.

"No," Roman said, and he pushed away Bernard's hand.

As they left the garage, Roman turned on the radio, and they sat for the hour back to Lincoln without speaking. Roman drove numbly, his mind a throbbing, static space. Over and over he felt the thrust of his arm, pushing away Bernard and his three dollars.

LUCY WAS IN A marvelous mood. She had spent the day shopping and planning for Christmas; the entire house carried the spicy, colorful scent of the impending holidays. She had made a wonderful dinner: roast lamb chops, potatoes, and string beans. They sat down at a table set with richly colored woven placemats and red napkins. Lucy lit the tall, pale candles. Roman's eyes stung. Again, he thought shamefully of the way he had shoved away Bernard's three dollars. For a long, curious moment, he felt he was, and had possibly always been, a stranger to this table—and that the table itself, with its thoughtful and delicious beauty, was now sealed in amber, sealed away from him.

"What's for dessert?" asked Avery, as he picked up his fork.

"It's a secret," Lucy said. "Why must you know?"

"I need to know how much room to save."

"You need to learn to live in the present."

"Is it in the oven?" he asked, glancing in the direction of the kitchen.

"If you sneak a peek, you forfeit an item from your stocking," she said cheerfully. "Sit down." She smiled at Bernard. "This child is absolutely glued to the commercial aspects of the holiday. You'll see."

Bernard looked up and said, very gently, "You've been so wonderful, but I feel quite strongly that I should leave your family's holidays to you, your privacy."

Avery looked up from his plate. "You're leaving?"

Lucy shook her head in dismay. "You can't leave now," she said. "Where will you go?"

"I've had a truly wonderful time with you," Bernard said, "and I will always be grateful for your generosity, but I think it's time that I returned to New York."

Roman sat listening to Avery protest and Lucy plead with Bernard to stay. She pointed out he was no trouble to them at all and questioned him about where he would next be living. Roman wanted desperately to blurt out the whole story, to bring up what had happened, but he held back.

More than anything, he wanted to talk to Lucy, wished for Lucy's reassurance that this was not his fault, but how could he seek her comfort when he suspected—when he was certain—that he was the reason for Bernard's deci- sion to leave? Moreover, Bernard's silence on the issue left him unsure how to go about it. This silence shamed Roman more than any complaint or conflict might have done. Over the next few days, as Bernard made ready to depart, Roman tried not to be alone in the room with him. The awkward- ness grew, until, on the day Bernard left town, he and Roman barely spoke.

———

ROMAN'S PUBLISHER accepted *An Imagined Life*. Roman's young editor, a recent graduate of the School, was effusive in describing how impressed she was by Roman's treatment of the subject matter. She wrote of mainstream reviews and an unusually large first printing, for a book of poetry. Roman felt somewhat disappointed. His editor seemed to think the book was notable not for its worth as poetry, but for the fact that his own mother had run away, and for "its sensitive exploration of the heretofore rarely visited subject matter of mother-son abandonment." He did not bother to protest; he felt separate from the poems now, as if they were the work of long ago.

The winter months passed, unaccountably dreary. After the holidays, Lucy was struck by an unknown malady or, more accurately, a mysterious and consuming fatigue. She seemed as tired when she woke as she had been when she went to sleep. She spent whole mornings sleeping, lingering in their bedroom until the afternoon, and when Roman entered she was not surrounded by books or even chatting on the telephone, but lying in bed with her eyes closed, or sometimes staring at the melting icicles outside the window. He persuaded her to see the doctor, but she showed no clinical signs of mono or other illnesses.

Roman, struck by a sense of foreboding he could not place, tried to nurture her. It was easy to take care of her now that she was still, contained. Her chilliness had abated, and she was pleasant to him, if preoccupied. She seemed to be chewing on a great thought. He brought her coffee and cereal in the mornings and made dinner for himself and Avery, and sometimes, when dinner was over, he came up and read her bits of news from the evening paper. At night he lay next to her unable to sleep, but he did not tell her of his anxiety. There was no comfort to be found in her. Some vital energy had evaporated; her hair and eyes were dull and her skin was drawn over her features. She insisted that she was not melancholic, only tired, and if he pressed too hard, she said she wanted to be left alone.

One morning in late March, after Avery had left for school, Roman went into the bedroom with a bowl of strawberries. He thought she might enjoy this sign of spring, the sight of the red berries in the blue and white bowl she had always liked. She was sitting on the side of the bed, her face pale and circles under her eyes. She started at his entrance, put her finger to her lips, and stared ahead out of the window as fiercely as someone who had been interrupted while reciting an epic verse from memory, or—he would think later—concentrating on the remnants of a dream.

"I don't care," she said. "You can put them in the fridge. Thanks," she added, and waved him away with a vague hand, as if she were a duchess in decline, and he her servant. Her vague gesture awoke a recognition from some layer of his mind. It was a gesture of such self-absorption, such indifferent dismissal of the world, that in a sober person it could be only a sign of falling into love, or out of love. He began to wonder if he had been fooled, absolutely; if, for months, he had missed what had been going on before his face.

"Do you miss Bernard?" he asked.

Lucy said, "I do." After a moment, she straightened and looked directly at Roman. "What did you say to Bernard to make him decide to leave?"

"I didn't say anything," said Roman. He crossed his arms over his chest. The day was very quiet; around them, the house echoed his words. "But I do think it was time for Bernard to go back to New York. Don't you?"

"He had nowhere to live."

"He was fine, as it turned out, with the housesitting gig you found for him."

"He was broke."

"He's too good for a regular job," said Roman acidly.

"He only pays seven hundred dollars a month for his apartment. If he left New York, he'd have had to give it up."

"What about little problems, such as saving for the day when he can't climb all those stairs anymore?"

"Why do you resent him so much?"

"You haven't noticed, Lucy? I'm a sellout to Bernard. I'm not living a life exalted enough for him. The air he breathes is far too pure for me."

"Please."

"I'm just a salaried drudge. If I were a true poet, I would take shit jobs and live off my friends, to support my art."

"Roman."

"Look," he said, "aren't you glad he's out of the house? It would make it easier for us to try again, for what you wanted."

He hoped Lucy might welcome his change of subject, but she was silent.

He went on. "Didn't you find it odd, to have Bernard in the attic, Bernard at dinner every night, Bernard in the morning nursing his cup of tea? Didn't you think it odd to have an extra presence, always, in the house? It was like having a ghost."

As he spoke, Lucy gazed at him, eyes lit, in a way that made him feel he had said something irretrievable.

"I suppose it was better for you," he said, awkwardly. "You and Bernard were close. You spent a lot of time with him."

She was silent for a moment. He could almost feel a drop in the air pressure in the room, and the soft morning light grew colorless with impending change.

Then Lucy said, "I'm beginning to think I do know what it's like to live with a third person in the house."

"What are you talking about?"

She was clenching the bedspread. Her face was suddenly alive again, her eyes dark and clear. "I've had a lot of time to think," she said. "Bernard talked a lot about the past while he was here. It got me to thinking about graduate school, and the rumors I heard then. Roman, what exactly happened between you and Miranda?"

He and Bernard had never discussed the affair, he had told no one; but he felt Bernard had betrayed him. "Bernard is full of shit," he said.

"He didn't say anything specific to me: don't blame him. It was you who made me think, the way that you shut down the conversation whenever he talked about our seminar, whenever he brought up Miranda's name."

"That was about ten thousand years ago, Lucy."

"Ten thousand years ago, there was nothing between the two of you?"

"It wasn't a big deal," he said. "It was just a physical thing."

No sooner had he spoken the words than he wished he could take them back.

"Just a physical thing," she said. Her face grew more alive, more vivid. But there was no trace of warmth, and a wrenched, angry scowl twisted her mouth. He moved backward, startled. He did not recognize her. "So I'm to understand," she said, "that you did more than *let her buy you dinner*."

He was stung by his own words, and by the exactitude of her memory. And yet, how could it matter now—something that had happened so many years ago, before he and Lucy had ever even kissed—after the thousands of nights they'd spent together, after the child, the house?

How could he have told her? His experience with Miranda lay contained, sealed away, in his memory. He was not sure what to make of what had happened, did not understand it himself, but he knew that it belonged to him.

"It has nothing to do with you and me," he said. "It was a long time ago."

"It has nothing to do with me."

"Why sure," he said, confused. His memory was heavy, its contents gleaming. "I had a—" He stopped, because he was not sure what to call it. "Just the way you did, with Max."

"You and Miranda were like me and Max Zabor."

He struggled, hard, against the impulse to not tell. But

the information had begun to spill from its container. "Not exactly. Sure, we made love, lots of times, if that's what you are trying to get at," he said. "But she was married then. And we were together less than six months."

"And you went to bed with me, in New York, when we were talking about Miranda, but you didn't tell me."

"It didn't seem an ideal subject at the time."

Lucy swallowed. "You're a rat, Roman," she said, quietly but distinctly.

"I haven't spoken to Miranda since before we were married," he said. "I should think that after everything, our relationship should hardly matter to you."

"So now you're saying it was a 'relationship'? Enough of a 'relationship' for her to choose you for a major prize?"

Roman felt the hair rise on his neck. He did not speak but turned to face her, aggrieved, insulted, daring her to keep going.

She gazed steadily back at him. She said, "Miranda suffered for that prize, I think. I don't know if she had the same influence after that."

"That's ridiculous," he snapped. "Professors give out prizes to their former students all the time, perhaps those they've slept with or those with whom they haven't."

"I'm not saying it was fair. The fact is that her reputation took a turn for the worse."

He guessed that these were the kinds of things others discussed, other former students of Miranda's when they occasionally spoke—things reminisced upon, dissected, mused over. The idea of these conversations, the casual solicitude, enraged him. He turned abruptly away from her. "You've said enough," he said.

"Now you're affronted. You think this is about *you*, Roman."

"No, clearly it's about *you*—you and whatever conversations you and Bernard were having while he was living off of us, in our house."

"You never understood that men and women can be friends," she said. "He is a very loyal person and a true poet. I don't think that you appreciate him or his work."

It was astonishing, that his admiration for Bernard's work could be so misconstrued and disregarded.

"I've always thought Bernard was loyal to his early fantasies of getting into your pants," said Roman. "Is that a privilege you reserve these days only for 'true poets'? And does he reserve his true friendship only for those who've failed to 'fulfill their early promise'?"

Lucy turned white. He had gone too far. Tears appeared in the corners of her eyes. He stood and began to pace the room, agitated and distressed, but also angry with her for being hurt.

"Do you want to know what I really think?" she asked.

"Go ahead," he said. He paced.

"I appreciate Bernard because he talks to me about my own work, as well as needing my support."

Roman turned to look at her. She sat on the edge of the bed, her face contorted, her fingers gripping the mattress. "You think I need too much support," he said.

"I think—yes. I think I'm tired of being supportive of

your work. Do you know how many thousands of times we've talked about you and your work?"

"Do you mean," he said, despite himself, "that all of these years, you've been lying?"

"Lying?" She was shouting now. "As in, telling a deliberate untruth? No. There are wonderful things about your poetry, Roman. But lying as in withholding? Perhaps. Perhaps I did. But if I did," she said, "if I did withhold my opinion, it was partly because you never asked. You never wanted to know anything except that it was wonderful."

His mind rang with the contempt and fury in her voice. "I thought you did think it was wonderful," he said. "From the beginning." He had one more point to make, one straw to grasp. "Even that day, in her class," he said, "so many years ago, you stood up against everyone to support my poems."

"Good Lord, Roman! Don't you know that for a woman to praise your work is the only way to get you to notice her at all?"

ROMAN WROTE TO BERNARD.

"Please don't discuss with my wife your judgments about my work or my relationships with our former teachers. I moved beyond graduate school some time ago, and I wish you would as well." He thought for a moment, and ended his letter, "I would appreciate it if you did not include my letters in your collection of correspondence with the writers of our age."

He had no idea how Bernard would respond. He had

always known that there was a flip side to Bernard's thought-fulness: had he not considered it that Thanksgiving afternoon so long ago, in inquiring about the contents of Bernard's file cabinets? The memory made him uneasy. A few weeks later, when he received a padded envelope from New York, return receipt requested, he recognized the handwriting. The package was clearly a manuscript, meticulously wrapped, its contents secured with string. Roman opened the package and cut the string.

There was a note: "I imagine you wish you'd never let me into your house. It must be true, that one should never mix debt and affection."

There was a folder. Roman opened it. Inside was a pile of letters, carefully smoothed flat, with envelopes clipped to the corners. They were all of the letters he had written to Bernard over the last sixteen years.

PART THREE

ALL IS FORGOTTEN,
NOTHING IS LOST

—

IN MAY 1673, THE MISSIONARY FATHER JACQUES MARQUETTE and the hunter and trapper Louis Joliet set off to explore the wilderness southwest of Quebec. They had been sent by their country and their Church: Joliet to claim new lands for the French Crown, and Father Marquette to convert inhabitants to the Holy Word. Marquette, an experienced traveler, recorded their trip. According to his journal, their group traveled in birch-bark canoes through what is now northern Michigan, portaging and paddling a watery path through what is now Wisconsin, until the day they reached the Mississippi.

Many have since believed Marquette and Joliet discovered the great river, but in truth, they only encountered it; for it had, of course, existed long before they reached it. How extraordinary a sight it must have been! Lush and wild and swollen on the brink of summer. Marquette wrote of the river's slow current and changing width; its myriad small islands, hidden whirlpools, and monstrous fish. He wrote of meeting the Illinois natives, who warned of savages to the south.

"I replied that I feared not death," he wrote, "and that I regarded no happiness as greater than that of losing my life for the glory of Him who has made all. This is what these poor people cannot understand."

Marquette's death came only two years later, during another New World exploration, of dysentery. No such knowledge exists of Joliet's death. Joliet, the failed seminarian turned adventurer and trader, would make his mark on this one trip. He would then vanish from our knowing, part of the story that has been left to the poets and historians.

When the poet wrote of the explorers at the mouth of the great river, he was seized by the recognition of his own failure as a man. His own faith fell to ashes beside theirs—their humility such that they thought nothing of their lives. For it is through humility, he knew, that holiness—and poetry—find entrance to the human soul.

Bernard had been working on his poem for decades when he began to understand how fervently he was attached to his own vanity, envy, and desire. Although they separated him from faith, these sins were all he had. He could not give them up, not even for God. On the riverbank, he knew he would never be worthy. How might God, all-knowing, and limitless, be expected to bother with his misshapen and pathetic soul— a soul twisted by its mortal end and beginning?

Historians have written that the land Marquette and Joliet explored was lost to France. The floodplain was turned into farmland, settled by Germans and Scandinavians. Perhaps the only sign of the French in Wisconsin today is the names they left behind, such as the name of Bernard's hometown, Fond du Lac, which means "bottom of the lake."

———

IT WAS ALMOST ten years after Roman's divorce. Late one night, while half asleep in a taxicab to his hotel from the Los Angeles airport, Roman caught a few words from the driver's radio. Its volume was turned so low he felt almost that he was eavesdropping. "—from his fifth-floor walk-up apartment in the East Village, the reclusive poet and literary correspondent of his generation," the reporter said. "Can you hear me?"

There was a faint pause, then the reply. The enunciation was precise, old-fashioned, and hauntingly familiar. "Yes, I hear you."

"We understand that you rarely leave your neighborhood," said the reporter. "Is this the reason you developed into a letter writer?"

Bernard—Roman understood only gradually that it was he—replied, "Perhaps that's true. I have always been a somewhat retiring person, whose social circle was quite small. Over the years, as my family in the Midwest has passed away one by one, and because the majority of the people whom I know live here in New York City, I find few reasons to travel. I'm also somewhat restricted by my circumstances. I don't drive. Moreover, I have lived what I would call a quiet life, and as a result, I have carried on most of my life adventures in an internal world. As a child, many of my most valuable experiences took place while reading novels and poems. When I grew up, it seemed necessary to contact the writers of those works. I discovered over time that these relationships had a tendency to develop into something that was quite valuable to me, so valuable that perhaps they fulfilled my need for the rush and flow of 'real life.'"

"How did you develop your avocation of what you call a 'pen pal'?"

"It began quite accidentally, with an adolescent fascination with the idea of living writers. It seemed extraordinary to me, and it still does, that on this earth exist a number of living poets and writers whose works inspire and excite readers as much as they did me. As a young man, I set about to write a series of 'letters of admiration,' as I have called them, to these poets and writers. I expected no response, but I was thrilled when I received a number of replies."

"One of those writers, we understand, was the late Pulitzer Prize–winning novelist, World War II hero, and Princeton alumnus John Valentine."

"Yes. I loved, and still love, his early novel, *Open Ends*. I wrote to him the year I first read the novel, in 1985."

"It was reported in the *New York Times* that the Princeton University Library has contacted you repeatedly about the possibility of their buying a collection of Valentine's letters that were written to you over a period of more than twenty years, before he committed suicide two years ago on the brink of publishing his internationally celebrated novel, *December Burning*," said the reporter. "Upon his death, the Library bought his other papers, in which have been discovered more than forty letters from you, implying that Valentine discussed in his replies his mortality, as well as the details of his writing life during the eighteen years in which he struggled to complete the novel. Why have you held on to Valentine's letters?"

"I feel that in my decision to keep the letters I am fulfilling an understanding I had with John," said Bernard. "He was a very private man. It seems to me that I would be making public what was once a private conversation."

"There has been enormous interest in John Valentine, not least because of the speculation of his having had a romantic affair with his lieutenant and mentor, the novelist Jonathan Tracey, when he was crossing the Atlantic to serve in World War II, and with whom he had a falling-out shortly before he married his wife, Joanne Acheson. Specifically, did Valentine discuss a physical affair with Jonathan Tracey in his letters?"

"I can't answer that," said Bernard gently.

"Aside from their potential to define this relationship, would you believe the letters are valuable?"

"In his crucial early years of development as a writer, Jonathan Tracey was a central figure in John's work, the teacher and reader who witnessed everything he wrote—as well as what he would not write. For these reasons alone, I do believe that the content of John's letters will be thought valuable, not only to writers and scholars but to all readers who seek to understand the struggles of the human condition."

"It would appear that you are now a keeper of secrets."

"I am, as it turns out," said Bernard. "And yet, if my habit of correspondence has taught me anything, it is that all of us keep secrets, even those of us whose literary habits oblige us to write down what we know. John believed it was essential for him to express a thought in words in order to know it at all. He once claimed that a wasted writer is one who spends his life pursuing false work in the hope of hiding from his own secrets. The luckiest writers cannot hide from them."

"What are your plans for your collection of letters?"

"I have no plans," said Bernard. "I am still in my fifties. I live a life in which my greatest risk-taking is crossing the street; although, I admit to being such a creature of habit that I tend to meet most of my needs within a five-block radius of my apartment." This was followed by a sound that at first sounded like laughter but might have been interference. "Therefore, I certainly don't expect—" The radio sputtered. "I suppose it's true, I will need plans—"

At that point, the taxicab passed into a valley and Bernard's words broke up entirely, dissolving into static.

When he returned home from Los Angeles, Roman tried to trace the interview, but he did not know the station. He searched for months, and even set his research assistant onto the task, but found nothing. He knew that it had been no dream. Bernard, of course, still existed; Bernard was living in New York City, in the rent-controlled apartment. For all these years, Roman had kept the address, and yet he could not bring himself to write a letter.

He spoke rarely to Lucy. He told himself that this was understandable, even predictable. He had at first assumed that, since they had parted with relative amicability, they would stay friends. In the months immediately following the divorce, they had spoken often on the phone, and then, later, less frequently. Lucy called to congratulate him when *An*

Imagined Life won the Pulitzer. She seemed genuinely happy for him. For several years, they maintained contact involving Avery. But when Avery entered Stanford, on a baseball scholarship, Lucy moved to Minneapolis. She had begun to write again, seriously this time, and she found someone to stage her play. She was accepted to some colonies, became a frequent guest at workshops, and, the previous year, had won a national grant for emerging artists. It was as if her creative gift had somehow lain dormant in their marriage, then flourished abundantly once he was gone. At some point in the last few years, Roman realized he was the one who always called her, and that she had in reality ceased to initiate contact shortly after Avery turned eighteen. By then Roman was settled firmly in his new job. He'd had brief relationships with other women. And yet, apart from student conferences, conversations on his travels, and negotiations with his editor, he seldom spoke to anyone. Despite this sense of isolation, he restricted his phone calls to Lucy thereafter.

His early dream for *An Imagined Life*—his dream that the book would make a life beyond Lincoln—had come to pass. That this life would be lived without Lucy, he had not imagined.

He was now as distinguished a poet as he had ever wished to be. The Pulitzer was one more bit of proof that he had reached a position beyond uncertainty. Proof that the Detweiler—the cause of such joy leading to such doubt—had not been given erroneously. He knew this, and yet somehow the doubt persisted.

His new job in California required almost no teaching.

He had the time to travel—and travel he did, mostly in the United States, but also to Europe and to other places he could have only dreamed that he would go. He met the men and women considered the great poets and patrons of his age. He slept in their houses and conversed with them over long dinners in the golden light of their vineyards. During this time, he found himself frequently imagining Bernard, in his apartment. An eternal drip of the bathroom sink that sounded throughout, only somewhat muffled by the piles of books upon the furniture Roman remembered from his single visit: a narrow bed, a desk, and the old figurine of Christ that had stood on Bernard's filing cabinet in Bonneville. Many other things had vanished from Roman's life: the house in Lincoln was sold, Lucy's quilts given away. Lucy herself was now living in a mysterious new world, an urban world of walk-in closets, bare white surfaces, and stainless-steel countertops. Even Avery's life seemed now shrouded in secret, hidden by geography.

But Bernard remained in New York. Since the conversation that had ended with Roman refusing Bernard's three dollars, Bernard had become a constant presence, a living voice in Roman's mind. "This isn't poetry," Bernard would say, when Roman found himself, upon a college visit, corralled into a late, exhausting dinner with wealthy donors to the school. "This isn't, not remotely, poetry," Bernard would announce, when Roman found himself on a board of advisors to a federal project to compose an inscription on a new monument. Bernard's presence was, at first, troubling; then, annoying; but after a few years, Roman came to accept it, welcome it, even to yearn for it at times. Whenever he stepped off a plane in some new place—for he gave many readings and lectures, traveling upon invitation—he left behind his latest stop with relief, and when he arrived in his new stop, often finding himself in an unpredictable, even queer, situation—for the organizations that requested Roman to read were a collection of the provincial, the distinguished, and the odd—he thought about what Bernard might make of this new place. More than once, while being driven along some unfamiliar highway somewhere in the interior of the continent, he recalled the images from Bernard's manuscript: the delicate, pale light of the north, the sky coruscating with migrating birds, the green earth sloping, tumbling, down to the great river. Images of a glorious, unforeseen new world that made him think of innocence.

He understood that he had, mysteriously and without consenting, reached a point in his life where such newness was gone from it; and he understood that it would not return. For no matter how many trips Roman made—to Berlin, to Rome, to Mexico City—he did not escape a life in which a world had ended, a life that he had survived alone, and from which he was now excluded. Something he had been waiting for, some powerful transcendence for which he had held his breath, would not take place. When had this opportunity for transcendence passed? Had he even paid attention?

A year after overhearing Bernard's interview, Roman was invited to give a reading at a small college in New Mexico. While glancing through the paper on the plane, he learned Miranda had died. The *New York Times* obituary reported it had been breast cancer. The article was primarily an assessment of her groundbreaking career as a poet, but it did mention that she had mentored many students in three decades on the faculty at the School, and there was a list of poets that included his name.

Roman read the article twice, then folded the newspaper and slipped it into the outer zip compartment of his carry-on suitcase. He rarely thought of Miranda now, and when he did, it was with an understanding that he had been, during those six months, very happy. He had known, since winning the Pulitzer, that he was required to take his place among the generation of elders. Now, with the death of his teacher, this was irrefutable.

Roman stepped off the plane. He walked across the tarmac toward the airport and the small group waiting to greet passengers; a faculty member named Phebe Hollander had been assigned to meet him. It was an afternoon in mid-November. Planes glittered, runways stretched to the horizon, burnished with the warm southwestern light. He was suddenly filled with a yearning for winter: for bare trees, for snow. A snowball in his hands, Miranda's laughter. A change settled into his heart: it was the weight of solitude. Whatever experience he and Miranda had shared, with its lingering sweetness and its memory of responsibility and shame, now belonged to only him.

When he emerged from the gate and looked for a placard bearing his name among the small crowd waiting for passengers, a woman cried, "Roman!" and the voice, familiar, coming from a face he did not recognize, stopped him short. It was Phebe Platz, now a professor of English.

Phebe had become a pretty woman of late middle age, her red hair dyed now, her breasts still set off by the décolletage of her flowing blouse. Roman was surprised that he felt so happy to see her, to see a familiar face where none had been expected.

While Roman gave his reading, with Phebe in the second row, he let his eyes wander over the audience in search of other faces he might recognize. On his travels, he met many poets, famous and obscure, and he met many readers of poetry. After his events, he was often approached by old acquaintances, and by strangers, admirers of his poetry. But a conversation with the one person he most wanted to see never came to pass. His mother did not appear. She had been a very young woman when she became lost to him, slender, with dark curls and a heart-shaped face. In the last few years, he had thought of her more and more frequently. How far had she gone?—as far, perhaps, as New Mexico. He had not the heart to trace her, and so waited for her to present herself to him, and she did not.

He went to dinner with several faculty and, afterward, out to drinks with Phebe in a bar filled with images of lizards and cacti and hieroglyphics from long-deceased pueblo dwellers. Phebe had married a biologist named Ralph Hollander and raised two daughters, both in college. Her husband had left three years before. The romantic attachment had worn itself out, she said. She was fairly certain that her ability to attach herself to any man had worn itself out along with the end of that relationship.

Roman understood. He was ashamed of the way he had

once striven with such scorn to overlook the fact that he and Phebe had ever been intimate. Why had he treated her with such dismissiveness? Because, he understood now, he had imagined for himself a future that did not lie with Phebe Platz. He had been correct. But he had also never foreseen that his life would take such a turn that a pleasant evening with an old acquaintance would mean something to him.

Somehow Phebe had managed, in the intervening years, to put her dislike of him behind. Her generosity made it possible for him to enjoy her company again.

She brought up the subject of Miranda's death; she had heard the news from Marlene, who was now married to a lawyer in Cambridge, Massachusetts. Roman said he had read the obituary and that he hadn't spoken to Miranda since a few years after graduation. Phebe let the matter pass, for which Roman felt grateful.

"I have a question for you," he said, changing the subject. "I know it's pathetic to bring up such buried bones, but why did you stop hating me?"

Phebe smiled. "I was young," she said, "and so were you. You were the most driven of us. You were so arrogant, so certain of yourself and your future. You turned out to be right, of course."

Roman imagined the young man that she described. He had been driven. He had been arrogant. "I was terrified," he said.

"I felt injured, I think, that I merited such a short pause on your part—such a brief pause from whatever you were heading for. I wanted life to teach you a lesson."

"Yes."

"I didn't know whether I'd stopped hating you—not until I saw you only a few hours ago, in the airport."

Roman nodded.

When Phebe later drove Roman back to his hotel, they parted with fondness.

The following morning, on the return flight, Roman was seated at the window. He watched the dark, flat blade of the wing cut through the clouds, then angle up into the sunshine. Phebe had understood: he was no longer to be hated. He knew, with a finality that crept upon him as imperceptibly as breathing, that he himself, in some undefinable moment, had passed that turning point when regret had overtaken expectation. When had this happened?

He could identify that moment only for others. He had not been present at Avery's playoff game at Stanford, but he could envision it perfectly, had imagined it a hundred times. An unusually warm, sunny afternoon in late April at Cardinal Stadium. Palm trees rustling in a dry breeze. Thousands of cheering spectators and major league scouts in the stands. It was the top of the eighth, with the score tied at 1–1 and a man on third as the result of a single and an error. Avery was finishing a successful junior year. He had thrown almost a hundred pitches, but he was still strong, his long legs and arms now disciplined to strength and perfect grace. He was focused on the batter, a formidable senior outfielder from UCLA.

What happened next Roman could not imagine without a fragmentary moment of disbelief. Avery delivered a fastball. The batter drove the ball straight back over the pitcher's mound, striking Avery above his right wrist. It was an infield hit, and scored a run. The trainers ran to the mound, and Avery left the game.

The team physician examined Avery and sent him to the hospital. The ball had broken his radius. The surgeon set it perfectly, with no complications. Lucy's voice over the phone was light and friendly with relief; Avery would pitch again the following season.

But as the months passed, the doctors became puzzled, then skeptical. Two X-rays revealed no real trouble, but no progress. It was a clean break that did not heal. More frequent X-rays brought moments of anxiety, then rage, and, finally, when Avery was speaking to his mother, tears.

Lucy called Roman, her own voice wobbling.

"How could we know he would have this problem? He never broke anything before, not even a finger. He led a charmed life. How were we to know?"

It was the first time that she had expressed need for him in years, and he could not answer the question she repeated.

Avery could not play baseball again. He took a quarter off and finished his degree, reconsidering. "I am looking for a Plan B," he wrote to Roman. "Do you remember, long ago, you told me that I should have a Plan B? Somehow, I felt that your advice didn't apply to me. I thought that if I just made baseball into the center of my life, if I cut out everything else, then baseball would come through for me. I don't know why I was so sure it would work. At least my grades are good—you made me study. I suppose I should be thankful."

That December, at winter graduation, Avery had

announced his news. He had been accepted into the Peace Corps. Plan B lay with his girlfriend in the country of her birth. Lucy beamed and nodded. Avery leaned his elbows on the table and looked at his plate. Roman watched his son's handsome, downcast face—his straight, even features concealing his confusion. He lacked the surety that had brought him to the mound that afternoon. Roman understood that Avery's heart was lost. Like any heartbroken man, he was going away. Roman suspected it might be several years before his son returned to America. He knew that the departure of Avery was, in actuality, a part of the aftermath: the aftermath of the family that had once sat down at Thanksgiving to charlotte russe.

Lucy did not seem concerned. "It's so dangerous, so far away. But I'm proud of him," she said to Roman after lunch, when Avery had gone to drop his girlfriend's family at the airport. "Aren't you proud that he thinks about those other than himself? It seems those conversations with Bernard made an impression on his adolescent brain."

"I guess they did," said Roman.

"And don't you think," Lucy said, "that Avery is the best part of us, of our marriage? That it was all worthwhile in the end because of Avery?"

Looking out the window at the coastline and the sky as his plane circled to land, Roman wondered: Did Lucy mean to say that the rest of it—all of the peaceful and productive years in the house in Lincoln—had not been worthwhile? Perhaps she was right. Their marriage had been, in so many ways, an experiment in hope on both parts, and it had ended as Phebe's marriage did, with that romantic notion exhausted. Roman remembered the afternoon long ago in Manhattan, under Lucy's comforter, when he had chosen not to tell her about his affair with Miranda. Should he have told her then, and gambled on the possibility that she might still have the generosity to go forward? He would have to continue without knowing the answer.

A MONTH AFTER Miranda's death, Shannon Bruno, a distinguished poet of the avant-garde, suffered an aneurism at the lion camp while taking an out-of-town visitor to the San Diego Zoo. She was only fifty-one, and the journal *Elision* published two elegies mourning her departure. In January, the brilliant, little-known poet and playwright Max Zabor jumped from the Long Island Ferry and perished in the frigid water of the Sound. No one elegized Max's death: Roman heard the news from Phebe, with whom he had kept in touch. He considered writing to Lucy, then thought the better of it.

The following autumn, arriving home from a trip to Phnom Penh to visit Avery, Roman picked up his mail and found, atop a pile of bills and manuscripts, a letter addressed in a cramped, familiar hand.

Dear Roman,

In the last several years, with your life having become almost a matter of public record, I have followed with great interest your career and your travels, and I wish

you a much overdue congratulations on your splendid
successes. I'm aware that our correspondence did not end
with good feeling. It is therefore with some hesitation
that I write, and with the assumption that you may have
moved on, but also with the assumption that you may
have kept some glimmer of interest in the companions of
your youth. The intervening years have passed peacefully
for me. I've finished my long poem and I have been con-
tinuing my correspondence with the existing writers of our
day. Many of those with whom I first exchanged letters,
those whom we discussed in school, have died long ago.

But all of this may not be perhaps of interest to you,
and it is not related to my reason for writing after such a
long time. I am writing to ask if you might find a day or
two to come to New York. Last summer, I was diagnosed
with lung cancer. My case was never optimistic, but in
the past few weeks, it has grown worse. Now the doctors
are saying that I have until about New Year's to get my
affairs in order. I'm aware that I'm selfish to ask you to
visit me. I understand if you're not able. If you can come,
please let me know. I would like it very much. I have a
telephone now. The number is 212-555-1288.

Bernard

It was one of those timeless autumns in Northern California when the leaves, rather than falling from the trees, turn
pale brown and cling to the twigs, fading in the golden light
of afternoon. In Minneapolis, it would be already evening,

dark and quite cold. He did not wish to call Lucy. She had *not* told him about Bernard's illness, and to call for information felt like begging. Yet, still, he was grateful to receive the letter. He had come to understand that he and Lucy had been among the very few people outside of his own dwindling family with whom Bernard had spent time in the flesh. Aside from his correspondence project, Roman and Lucy were the only close friends Bernard had ever had. Certainly, Roman was the only person from whom Bernard had ever felt the need to cut off contact. Not a week passed by when Roman did not berate himself for allowing the friendship to end. How pointless it had been not to write back with some excuse, and ask for Bernard's forgiveness. And yet during all those years he could not, would not, be the first to write. How meaningless it was, and how strange, how peculiarly isolated Roman's own life had become.

A week later, he stood in the doorway of Bernard's hospital room at St. Vincent's.

He had heard Bernard on the phone—knew that his voice was now a wheezing sound, not quite a whisper: he had steeled himself against this reality—but when he entered the hospital room, he found that he had not adequately prepared himself.

Bernard was smiling his wide, innocent smile, but there was no more color in his face, and almost nothing to it, nothing but bones.

Roman could not help exclaiming, "But Bernardo, you never smoked."

"My parents both smoked like fish," Bernard said. His voice was gone, but he spoke with the same polite exactitude

Roman remembered. "Everybody did. Everyone who worked at the paper mill in Fond du Lac, that is." He stopped talking and took a long breath. On his wasted features, his irony took on a macabre, stripped-down glory. Roman, to his dismay, found himself smiling ironically in return.

Bernard went on. "Lucy said, with an uncharacteristic lack of sympathy, that they should be punished for child abuse, but, alas, they've been dead for twenty years."

Roman missed Lucy terribly. He wished that Lucy were right there, in this room with them. She would know what to say to Bernard, how to behave. She would be generous, not frightened. "How is Lucy?" he asked automatically.

"She came to visit me at my apartment, two weeks ago," said Bernard. "She's doing well."

"I'm glad," said Roman, half hoping that Bernard would change the subject. He had often wondered if it would be possible, after everything, to recover the friendship he and Lucy had shared at the beginning of their time together. But he suspected that without the presence of Bernard— without Bernard's encouragement in some way—it would be impossible.

"She stopped by on her way to Florence. Since she'll be gone three months, she wanted to make sure to see me"— here Bernard glanced at Roman, and there was a curious look in his eyes, a look Roman could recognize as a sympathy that arose from true dispassion—"before she left the country."

Roman found little consolation in the fact that he had been the one to make plans, if only plans to aim for immortality; while it was Bernard who had never planned for the future. Somehow, Bernard was accepting this ending as he had accepted other things: Bernard had seen it coming. It was Roman who had not. They would say goodbye. In half an hour, he would leave the room; he would say, "See you around, Bernardo," and it was unlikely they would meet again.

"Do you remember," Bernard was saying, "that Thanksgiving? The first Thanksgiving, the one we spent in my apartment?"

The smell of burnt cheese sticking to Bernard's flatiron; the pigeons scuttling and cooing in the eaves. "You said that you had found your One Great Reader," Roman said.

Bernard smiled, faraway. "I did."

Again, Roman failed to ask who the reader had been. It was suddenly more important that he tell Bernard what he was thinking at that moment. "Do you know what?" Roman said, "I never thought about having One Great Reader."

"Why did you write poetry, then?"

Why do we want to fall in love? Why do we want to pray? "I think," Roman began, with a sudden moment of gratitude that it was to Bernard he was speaking, that he could still talk to Bernard. Despite their falling-out, he counted on Bernard. An unexpected silence awaited him, a silence of many years. "I think that I wrote because I wanted there to be One Great Judge," he said. "I wanted the One Great Judge to find my work to be the best, the most brilliant, and to declare me the greatest poet of my time."

Bernard nodded. "Well, it happened, in some ways, didn't it?"

Roman shook his head. He wanted to complete this thought, and he had not been able to do it alone. He tried again. "But as time went on—at some point—" When had it been? "—I didn't even know it, but I stopped believing in the existence of that One Great Judge. And so I had no more reason to write poetry. Yet I've nothing else to do, except write poetry. Something is missing from me and from the poems, something lacking. But no one notices it, hardly anyone can see it, or perhaps, no one cares. And it turned out that there was no One Great Judge. And then I began to wish"—he took a breath—"to wish that I could have kept that ignorance, that innocence, I suppose. The innocence that drove me to work. It was something I failed to understand, to appreciate so long ago, in graduate school."

"At the seminar table," Bernard said, and smiled.

"Maybe if I had spent more time smoking, with the others." Roman tried to smile back.

"No," said Bernard. Roman remembered that Bernard had loathed the smell of cigarettes. "We learned a lot, as it was," Bernard said.

"We did," said Roman. He remembered the wise, biting, and wrongheaded things they had all said about the great writers of the past and present. The intensity of their discussions of each other's work. A thin, aggrieved voice entered his mind, *The use of language evinces a want of character*. And Phebe, years later, saying, *I wanted life to teach you a lesson*. He heard, suddenly, Miranda's low, musical tones. *Whom would you rather be? The one who desires? Or the object of desire?* Beneath the contempt, the seemingly indifferent instruction with its emphasis on large things: even with his poisonous envy and small-heartedness, he had indeed learned a lot. The most important moments of his life had passed without him knowing them.

Bernard's words broke a long silence. "Look, I never returned that copy of *Flight* that I borrowed from you in Lincoln."

"No problem," said Roman automatically, then for several seconds he could not remember what book Bernard was talking about.

"I apologize," said Bernard.

"It's fine," Roman said. The collection from the attic had been moved to California; many volumes had been misplaced along the way.

And yet Bernard looked troubled, searching for words. "I wanted to send it back for years. After we stopped talking." He paused and examined his hands. "But somehow I never did."

Roman studied Bernard, who was still struggling to speak, and understood he should say nothing.

"I want to tell you this," Bernard said, finally. "I envied you—that book. That's why I held on to it for so long. But now, of course, it won't give me any pleasure where I'm going. And I don't want it to be sold along with everything else, to pay my debts." Another wasted, glorious smile. This time Roman did not have the strength to smile back.

"You'll probably laugh to hear this," Bernard continued, "or perhaps you already know, but I had quite an attachment to Miranda."

"An attachment?" Roman repeated dully.

"Oh, I was in love with her," Bernard said. "I fell in love with her in school, and I was in love with her until she died." He paused, waiting for some kind of reply, and when Roman did not speak, he added, with his usual timid, faintly detached cheerfulness, "You probably find me ridiculous."

"Of course not," said Roman. He was suddenly envious of Bernard in a way that felt almost unendurable. But he understood now that he must endure it, that he must wait to hear what Bernard had to say.

Bernard took another long breath. "That spring, of graduation, I used to wake up early in the morning—three o'clock, four o'clock. I couldn't sleep. I would walk through her neighborhood. That's how I knew. You were always so careful, but almost every time I found your car, somewhere nearby. Never at the house, but nearby."

Roman remembered parking his car in the maze of roads and backyard alleys near Miranda's neighborhood and walking through the silent streets, very late, after the bars closed down: the fragrance of the night; his private mapping of the silent cats, the birds, the squirrels in their nests; and that thrum of his secret, vivid life in his fingertips—the open, alive, hungry feeling he had every time he had been away from Miranda and needed to go to her again. For a moment the feeling came back to him like the taste of a first sorrow, with such force that he could not breathe.

"Bernardo," he said, "did you ever talk to her about it?"

"Once," Bernard said, and looked more cheerful. "I was able to tell her before she died. She became more and more private, near the end. Sometimes when I'd try to call, she wouldn't answer her phone. But I went one last time to visit her in Bonneville. It was several years ago, when I had just learned she was ill. I said, 'I have been in love with you since graduate school but never had the courage . . . I don't want anything from you but I do want you to know.' She was lovely about it, really. She smiled her most beautiful—in that delightful way she had, and she said, 'Bernard, your friend-ship, more than any other in my life, has been a great source of support and a great solace.'" Bernard looked directly at Roman. "As I was saying, I envied you there, for a while. That was wrong. I'm sorry."

"Forget about it," Roman said. Bernard's words, and Miranda's, pierced him.

"It took me years to understand. For a long time I was ashamed. Then after she died, I felt regret I hadn't done more. But now I'm grateful to have loved her. Inadequate love is love. Unrequited love is love. I was lucky."

"Yes," Roman said. He swallowed, wishing that Bernard would stop, but now Bernard was getting up on his elbow, an action that betrayed a frightening thinness of his chest and trembling in his arms, while taking long drags of air with his ruined lungs, and he was reaching under his pillow—under his pillow! Roman had to look away—to pull out the copy of *Flight*. "Nurses always putting my stuff where I can't find it," he explained.

Roman reached out and took the book. "Thanks," he said, words inadequate to the end.

He made up his mind and tried again. "I'm in a hotel near

midtown," he said. "I'll try to rebook my ticket and my room for the next couple of weeks"—he hesitated—"in case you need anyone."

It was painful to look into Bernard's face, but he did.

"Thank you," Bernard said, meeting his gaze with that blue clarity. "Thank you, Roman."

In the taxi, Roman read the poems of Miranda's early solitude. The poetry jumped out at him again: her stark, exquisite lines and phrases. For all of her fame at one point, fewer readers turned to her work these days. Lucy had been right: her reputation was diminished. For one thing, she had never written poems exploring history or politics, never written on any subject other than experience. Her collections were considered beautiful, but slight. Moreover, the prevailing aesthetic had shifted toward the theoretical writing she had once condemned, and her work had been labeled "confessional" by the current crop of poets. It was astonishing, what could be forgotten. If her work had had a champion, someone from a younger generation perhaps, she might have better stood the test of time, but none of the acolytes had risen to that stature. She had only had Bernard. Bernard had taken good care of the book. The dust jacket was almost untouched, showing slight wear only in the corners, and the pages were unmarked. Roman closed the book, then opened it again and found on the title page, in Miranda's handwriting so familiar from long ago, the inscription. "For dear Roman, with admiration, veracity, and love."

Flipping the page, Roman found his old photograph of his class posed under a tree. The film had been exposed to too much light and everyone looked dazed and pale, undefined. Some of the group he no longer remembered and those he knew well were almost unidentifiable in their youth. Roman saw Lucy, vibrant and unembittered, smiling with a radiance that took his breath away. There was Bernard, almost boyish, and there, Roman saw, he himself stood in the back row beside Miranda. He barely recognized his straight, narrow body, the winged shoulders and luxuriant dark hair. He had the thoughtless grin of a young man bare-chested in the bow of a sailboat, an absolutely confident young man about to come into his inheritance—not an inheritance of money, he saw now, but of poetry. There could be no higher privilege and its price was sadness. He no longer knew this younger self; but he saw, with a bolt of grief, that he still knew Miranda. Miranda wore white and her hair lay like a cloud against her shoulders. It was clear that she had passed her youth, but the sight of her was heart-stopping. She stood with her head tilted close to his as if sharing a thought, wearing a dazzling smile of almost unbearable pride and happiness—pride and happiness for him, Roman. He understood now that she had given him the Detweiler out of love. He found a dim memory of the two of them holding hands throughout the picture-taking. Then hadn't they sneaked into an upstairs room in a strange house, in order to punish themselves once more for their inconvenient attachment? And hadn't he told her then that he was leaving town? He had not allowed her to accompany him to the airport.

Roman put the book away. His eyes and throat were full and dry, stopped up by dust. He felt a tearing need to speak to her; he longed to put his head next to hers so that she would comfort him in the way that she had once done. He wished to beseech her forgiveness and to hear her reassurances. He had meant the world to her. He had been cruel to her, and now there was nothing left of either love or cruelty except this image, with the faces pale as scars, burning into his memory. And as the taxi carried him downtown, a multitude of people passed—businessmen and dog walkers and young girls wearing their first high heels—and none of this mattered to them, of course, it would not matter to anyone else. For each of us, he understood, is born into our own time and eventually the things we held as the center of the world, dearly, unforgivingly, must fade.

BERNARD DIED EARLY the next week. He left behind a bank account with three hundred and five dollars, which, along with eight hundred of Roman's money, was enough to pay the final month's rent on his apartment and to persuade the landlord to release the seven boxes of manuscripts and twenty-four boxes of correspondence with the great writers of his age; and to release his mail, which contained a written offer, from Farrar, Straus, to publish his long poem. In his will, he named Roman and Lucy his literary coexecutors and bequeathed any future proceeds from his work to the Church.

ACKNOWLEDGMENTS

THIS NOVEL WAS COMPLETED DURING TWO SEMESTERS OF academic leave made possible by the John Simon Guggenheim Memorial Foundation and the University of Iowa. I am grateful to the Ucross Foundation for its precious gift of solitude and time. I am also indebted to my colleagues on the faculty of the Iowa Writers' Workshop, and in particular to Connie Brothers and James Alan McPherson, for their generosity in Fall 2008 and 2009.

My interest in poetry and poets is that of an outsider. The seeds of this interest were planted over a dozen years ago during a joint poetry-fiction workshop at Stanford University. My questions about art and teaching have developed over time in part from listening to conversations, in and out of class, at Iowa and at Warren Wilson College. Over the years, many poets and fiction writers at these three institutions have helped me explore the issue of how writing can be taught, and I am grateful to all of them for their wisdom and knowledge.

I would like to thank Eileen Bartos and Nan Cohen for their encouragement throughout the writing of this book, and Andrea Bewick, Ling Chang, Craig Collins, and Elizabeth Rourke for their invaluable readings. Stacey D'Erasmo and D. A. Powell provided precious insight. I am also indebted to James Galvin, Benjamin Hale, Ron Hansen, CJ Hribal, Bea Jacobson, Tyrone Geronimo Johnson, Andrew Stallings, Peter Turchi, Jan Weismiller, and the University of Iowa Libraries.

Once again, I would like to thank Jin Auh, Sarah Chalfant, and Jill Bialosky for their generous and long-standing support of my work.

Finally, I am grateful to Margot Livesey, whose brilliance as a writer and teacher has been a guiding example to me for many years.

ALL IS FORGOTTEN, NOTHING IS LOST

Lan Samantha Chang

ALL IS FORGOTTEN, NOTHING IS LOST

Lan Samantha Chang

DISCUSSION QUESTIONS

1. Roman notes that Miranda's persona at home is very different from her persona in the classroom. What do you make of this? How do characters in the novel change when they are in public, as opposed to when they are in private?

2. Bernard speaks of his desire for One Great Reader. What do you think he means by that? Does he ever find one? Do all of the characters have a Great Reader of their own?

3. Miranda says she "wouldn't marry a true poet, wouldn't trust a true poet farther than I could throw him." What does she mean by "true poet," and why are they so untrustworthy? Are any of the characters in *All Is Forgotten, Nothing Is Lost* true poets?

4. Early in the novel, Bernard wonders "what might be learned from the indifference of a great poet." Is this part of what drives his correspondence project? What do you think Bernard gains from his letters to the "writers of our time"?

5. Roman keeps a note on his desk that reads, *All that matters is the work.* How do different characters interpret this edict? What do you make of the fact that Lucy doesn't work during her marriage to Roman?

6. Roman tells Miranda that it was inappropriate for her to give him the Detweiler Award after their relationship. Do you agree? How would you have reacted?

7. The title *All Is Forgotten, Nothing Is Lost* comes from Bernard's long poem of the same name, about the expedition of Marquette and Joliet. What do the story and themes of the poem have in common with the novel?

8. Most of the characters in this novel are artists; Avery, with his promising baseball career, is the exception. How is Avery's involvement with baseball different than his parents' with poetry? How are the two pursuits similar?

9. The book seems to offer two models of poetic life—Bernard's and Roman's. How do these two ways of being a poet work? Are there more than two paths available? Where do Lucy and Miranda fit in?

10. At one point while in school, Roman wonders what his grandmother "would have made of the discussions in that evening's seminar." What do *you* think his grandmother would have made of the discussion? Do you think the conversations that Lucy, Roman, and Bernard have are important to people without a poetic background, or are they strictly technical?

11. The novel ends with a posthumous offer of publication for Bernard's long poem. What do you think Bernard would have made of it? Did Bernard want to be remembered, and if so, how, and by whom?

Pam Houston	*Sight Hound*
Helen Humphreys	*Coventry*
	The Lost Garden
Wayne Johnston	*The Custodian of Paradise*
Erica Jong	*Sappho's Leap*
Peg Kingman	*Not Yet Drown'd*
Nicole Krauss	*The History of Love**
Don Lee	*Country of Origin*
Ellen Litman	*The Last Chicken in America*
Vyvyane Loh	*Breaking the Tongue*
Benjamin Markovits	*A Quiet Adjustment*
Joe Meno	*The Great Perhaps*
Maaza Mengiste	*Beneath the Lion's Gaze*
Emily Mitchell	*The Last Summer of the World*
Honor Moore	*The Bishop's Daughter*
	The White Blackbird
Donna Morrissey	*Sylvanus Now**
Daniyal Mueenuddin	*In Other Rooms, Other Wonders*
Patrick O'Brian	*The Yellow Admiral**
Samantha Peale	*The American Painter Emma Dial*
Heidi Pitlor	*The Birthdays*
Jean Rhys	*Wide Sargasso Sea*
Mary Roach	*Bonk*
	*Spook**
	Stiff
Gay Salisbury and	
Laney Salisbury	*The Cruelest Miles*
Susan Fromberg Schaeffer	*The Snow Fox*
Laura Schenone	*The Lost Ravioli Recipes of Hoboken*
Jessica Shattuck	*The Hazards of Good Breeding*
	Perfect Life
Frances Sherwood	*The Book of Splendor*
Joan Silber	*Ideas of Heaven*
	The Size of the World
Dorothy Allred Solomon	*Daughter of the Saints*
Mark Strand and	
Eavan Boland	*The Making of a Poem**
Ellen Sussman (editor)	*Bad Girls*

Sara Stockbridge	*The Fortunes of Grace Hammer*
Barry Unsworth	*Land of Marvels*
	Sacred Hunger
Brady Udall	*The Lonely Polygamist*
Brad Watson	*The Heaven of Mercury**
Jenny White	*The Abyssinian Proof*
Belle Yang	*Forget Sorrow*

*Available only on the Norton Web site: www.wwnorton.com/guides